Love's Escape

My amazing
critique partner,
you're heaven-sent!
Blessings,
Carrie

This book is a work of fiction. Names, characters, places, and incidents are either products of the author's imagination or used fictitiously. Any similarity to actual people, organizations, and/or events is purely coincidental.

ISBN: 978-1-7366875-3-6

All rights reserved. No part of this publication may be reproduced or transmitted for commercial purposes, except for brief quotations in printed reviews, without written permission of the publisher.

Love's Escape © 2017 by Carrie Fancett Pagels
Second edition 2022

Published by Hearts Overcoming Press, USA

Front cover design by Carpe Librum Book Design,
www.carpelibrumbookdesign.com

Love's Escape

by

Carrie Fancett Pagels

Hearts Overcoming Press

James River Romances Series
Other Books in this series:

Dogwood Plantation
~Available in audiobook, ebook, and paperback

Return to Shirley Plantation
~Available in audiobook, ebook, and paperback
A Civil War bestseller on Amazon

The Steeplechase
(A Holt Medallion finalist)
~Available in ebook and paperback

ENDORSEMENTS

Carrie Fancett Pagels's 20+ books have received endorsements from some of the top authors in Christian Fiction:

Tracie Peterson, Suzanne Woods Fisher, Jen Turano, Carrie Turansky, Tamera Alexander, Julie Lessman, Susanne Dietze, Sarah Ladd, Serena B. Miller, Kathleen L. Maher, Jocelyn Green and more!

DEDICATION

In memory of Avis Fretz,
who was a fantastic teacher,
encouraging and nurturing my childhood creativity.

&

To my husband and children:
Jeffrey D. Pagels, Clark J. Pagels, and
Cassandra Rose Pagels Byrnes
What a blessing you are!

Prologue

Burwell Plantation
Charles City, Virginia 1848

Exquisite. That was the only word Nathan could summon to mind as he spied Phebe Burwell's companion, a shy looking woman with a striking visage.

"Welcome to our annual picnic, Mr. Pleasant." Mister Burwell stepped forward and slapped his back so hard that had Nathan been a less robust man he may have stumbled.

Nathan extended his hand and made sure he gripped Burwell's own with an iron grip that the man almost, just barely, began to wince.

The plantation owner made a habit of trying to intimidate guests, right from the start, so Nathan had planned to give the older man a bit of his own medicine. Sweat broke out on the older man's head.

Burwell wiped his brow. "Phebe's gonna be all excited that you made it here."

But it wasn't sixteen-year-old Phebe who'd captured Nathan's attention. Phebe's friend stood a small distance back from her, hands clasped demurely at her waist, her gown simple but not distracting from her beautiful features. "I'll go and make my greetings."

Burwell nodded then turned as other neighboring plantation owners, the Carters, strode forward. Their nearby home, Shirley Plantation, was older and more prosperous—something that always seemed to irritate Burwell. Today was no exception, as the man immediately altered his direction away from them, his nose wrinkled as though he'd smelled something foul then strode off. Why did the man keep inviting the Carters, then? Maybe in hopes of one day making a family connection via one of his daughters marrying a wealthy Carter son. If so, then Burwell might wish to try a little harder to be civil to the family.

Nathan puffed out a breath, then headed toward the young women. Sunlight broke through the clouds and shone reddish strands on Phebe's friend's auburn hair, which had been curled and pinned up in a plain style. There was something about her humility, and a pain he'd seen in her eyes, that drew him to the stranger. Surely, in his spirit, something tugged in a kind of recognition.

Someone pinched his neck and Nathan jumped. He swiveled to see who'd grabbed him.

His chum, David Bryant, guffawed. "I saw you staring at young Phebe. Don't let Burwell catch you."

It wasn't Burwell's daughter who Nathan was eying, but he wasn't going to correct his friend. "I see you made it in one piece—even though you weren't traveling with me." Truth be told, he'd have enjoyed his friend's company on the trip over. But David could get himself into the worst situations when he was traveling on land. Put him on a boat, though, and all was well.

David shrugged. "I had a visit to make over at the Flowers' place."

Nathan gritted his teeth. He truly worried for David, who was known for his rash behavior. The Flowers, a Quaker family, were on Father's list of abolitionist sympathizers. "Take care."

Love's Escape

One must be truly cautious, unlike David, when socializing with those who were bucking Southern plantation owners' ways.

"Don't I always?" A muscle jumped in his cheek. "And I'll blame your father if I get caught."

Father. Nathan gritted his teeth. Recently Father had a bee in his bonnet about the slaves in Virginia. A swarm actually, since one month earlier when his father had witnessed something at the Richmond wharf. Their family didn't own slaves, but they did have some freed men who worked at their business.

"Hasn't your father always emphasized that there are no differences among the races?"

Nathan nodded. "Indeed, that's how I was raised." What he believed.

"And hasn't he decried how the Indians are treated?"

"Yes, but they have enslaved each other, too."

David sighed. "That's not the point."

"I know, I know. It's what we're willing to do about it." Now that he was finished with his studies, Nathan had more time to consider what his father believed. And to wonder about all the secret meetings that went on in their home after hours. Those were no Bible study sessions being held in the parlor. Religious study groups didn't need guards posted at the street and at the front door and the parlor. Indeed, Nathan had been assigned as a look-out recently—a sign that the members might soon extend him an invitation into their society.

"I am about to be admitted to the Daffodil Study Group." David's voice held a mocking tone.

Nathan raised his eyebrows. "The *what*?"

"Your father is starting a *new* group." David rocked on his heels.

"Horticulturists? Since when had that interested him?"

"He feels this is an in-depth way to till the *soil* and make changes that could be long lasting."

David wasn't speaking of flowers.

Nathan swallowed hard. "Beneida is such a fleur?" David was playing with fire by sneaking around to meet with the young slave woman.

"Indeed."

"But these daffodils are being grown on *others'* soil." Mean-spirited men who thought nothing of filing suit if someone dared interfere with their *property*. "Which means one must exercise great care in interfering with that growth." Still, it must be done, although David wasn't the best choice for such secretive work.

"More like stifled than grown. Trampled. Ill-used and abused." David's nostrils twitched in distaste.

A group of young bucks, including Phillip Paulson III, Nathan's college friend, clustered around Phebe and her companion. "I thought the Paulsons were moving their horse ranch to the Shenandoah Valley?"

"They are. Joining up with the Davis family—the ones with not only gorgeous horses in their stables but also those foxhounds that are so prized by every family in the Commonwealth."

"Except ours. We're more cat people, if there is such a thing." Father had even asked one of his British friends to bring him one of his new breeds on his next trip over.

David guffawed. "Your father would never allow a foxhound to grace his home."

"True. Nor would his big tabby cat."

"You mean overgrown fur pillow." David had sat on Clancy a few too many times and felt the animal's sharp claws in his backside.

"Clancy wouldn't tolerate a canine in the house."

Love's Escape

"Yet another reason why I consider your family unconventional."

"If my father's pals in England have their way, you'll find more households keep felines as pets, not just as mousers."

Rolling his eyes heavenwards, David turned to face where young men chatted with Phebe but ignored her beautiful friend, uneasiness stirring in him.

"Come on." David jerked a thumb toward the table. "Let's join the others."

Long wooden tables lay covered with all manner of barbecued meats, breads, vegetable cassoulets, pies, cookies, punch, and more. Martha Paulson, his friend's lovely grandmother, shot a disapproving glance at her husband as he served himself an extra slice of buttermilk pie. "It won't be the same in Tidewater without the Paulsons."

Frowning, David leaned in. "They and the Davis family understand what it means to act upon their beliefs."

Nathan stiffened. "Friend against friend, family against family—that's what things are coming to now, isn't it?"

"Indeed, but not us two."

"Never."

David's stomach growled. "I haven't eaten all day."

"Surely you've become used to that at sea?"

"Oh no." He laughed. "I'm rarely seasick. And as captain, I'm accustomed to being fed heartily and only the best."

Nathan shook his head but followed David over to the groaning table. "I see you've not applied that same principle to your wardrobe, though." His friend's plain clothing was well-made but not stylish.

His friend laughed and removed his soft flat hat as they approached the others. "Good day."

Phillip Paulson grinned at David. "Lovely day, isn't it?"

"Perfect weather for the daffodils to glisten brightly in the sun." Martha Paulson smiled, as she turned to face Phebe and her friend.

Did she mean what he thought she implied? Nathan swallowed hard. That young woman couldn't possibly be a slave here. Could she? There was a young girl in Richmond whose owner, a judge, was becoming the topic of much discussion amongst the abolitionists. It was rumored that an image of her was being sent to the North, to stir up sympathies because the child, with her blond hair, blue eyes, and light skin clearly was the result of generations of white owners contributing to her lineage. Multi-generational sin was what father called it, and Nathan agreed.

David loaded up his plate. "Right now, I'm more interested in trying some of this barbecued pork. Did you bring your famous cornbread, Mrs. Paulson?"

The petite woman blushed. "I did. It's under that netting right there." She inclined her head toward the table's end.

"Good to see you boys. I'll catch up with you later, David, before you go." Paulson, a tall, elegant man with a thick mane of silver hair, reminded Nathan of his own father. Both good men. Both of them risking their lives on a cause close to their hearts. Was Nathan ready to take that step forward?

"Count on it." David shoved half a sugar cookie into his mouth and Martha Paulson giggled like a young girl as she and her husband moved away.

Nathan took only a ham biscuit, along with a drink. The trip over the rumbling roads from nearby Richmond had roiled his stomach. However, the nuanced dance he'd had to perform with Burwell and his cronies was likely the culprit. He followed David to beneath a tall Catalpa tree.

Love's Escape

"I have ended my courtship of the Paulson's granddaughter." David swiped a crumb from his jacket.

"I thought she was your cover." For David's forbidden relationship with Beneida, so it would be assumed he was pursuing a marriage. Nathan had never agreed with the deception, but David hadn't listened.

"Methinks your friend, Phillip the third, may have hinted to her that such was the case."

"I certainly didn't tell him." Although, to be honest, Nathan had given broad hints. His cheeks warmed and he bit into the savory ham biscuit.

"Regardless, I may need another young lady in these parts to become my new love interest—or rather my faux interest." David scooped a huge spoonful of meat and rice into his mouth.

Nathan huffed a sigh. "A handsome and wealthy sea captain and you worry about finding another belle to court?"

"I didn't say that," David said around his mouthful of food. He swallowed. "I just need to find a fake one soon."

"All right, all right." Nathan sipped his punch. Warm. And slightly sour. He swallowed it down hard.

The crowd around Phebe Burwell dispersed, leaving the two young women standing alone. "Do you know who that is with Phebe Burwell?"

Eyebrows pulling together, David briefly scowled in Phebe's direction. Just as quickly, a slight smirk pulled at his full lips. "Were you wanting to meet her?" He tossed back the contents of his cup.

A muscle jumped in Nathan's cheek. "Certainly. She's the most beautiful woman I've seen on my trips here." Anywhere, in fact.

David clapped him on the back. "That's because you've not yet set eyes on Beneida."

"Don't speak of such things too loudly." Nathan glanced around. "You may, as captain of your ship, be accustomed to running things, but around here, these plantation owners have their own ways of doing things." Much as he despised the practice of slavery, Nathan wasn't sure he had his friend's boldness to embrace abolitionism by secretly meeting with a beautiful young slave.

"You're right. But do let's get an introduction to Miss Burwell's. . . companion." David strode off and Nathan hurried to catch up with the long-legged man.

"Miss Burwell," Nathan called out as they neared the tall, flowerless Magnolia tree under which the woman stood with her pretty, auburn-haired companion. "How lovely to see you out in society."

Fluttering her eyelashes, the young miss dipped a curtsey. "Mother says I'm quite old enough. She came out, in London, when she was younger than I am."

"Younger than sixteen?" David asked, his tone skeptical.

"Yes."

Phebe extended her hand and David bent over it, one hand behind his back, and kissed it. Phebe's eyes narrowed. "You might wish to follow Mr. Pleasant's attire the next time you're out in society, Mr. Bryant."

David straightened, chuckling. "I'm not inclined toward stripes and braided trims."

Miss Burwell focused her attention on Nathan. "Look how well his tan and blue bias-cut waistcoat goes with those matching stripes, though."

David closed one eye hard. "If I wore anything like that near the docks, my men would toss me over into the water."

"Well, you're not by the docks, now, are you sir?" Phebe playfully swatted at him with her closed fan.

"Indeed, I am not." David smiled and bent at the waist.

The green-eyed beauty standing behind Phebe locked gazes with Nathan. When he smiled at her, she blushed and looked away.

"Nathan, come say hello to Miss Burwell." David waved him on.

Nathan stepped forward and kissed Phebe's hand. "Delighted to see you, Miss Burwell."

Then, he looked past their hostess to her friend. Phebe must have caught him because she scowled and turned around.

"Girl! Go and fetch us some of that cold lemonade from the icehouse."

"Yes'm." The other woman turned on her heel and fled.

Nathan's gut clenched.

David leaned in. "I take it that's your new house slave?"

Nathan's breath caught in his throat.

Phebe waved her hand. "Not new. Lettie's been with us forever."

Born into slavery then. Her skin was no darker than Phebe's and her eyes lighter. On any city street she could have passed for white.

"But she's usually taking care of Nanny."

Nanny Burwell was the elderly matriarch of the family. Nathan had spoken with her recently when she came to Richmond to plan her own funeral arrangements. She was a feisty old woman and had invited Nathan and David to this big picnic that her family was throwing to celebrate another successful harvest. And here they were.

"Lettie's mammy has been here since before I was born. Works in the kitchen house and made half the food that's out here on Mama's china platters."

David nodded. If Nathan didn't know any better, he'd think his friend was agreeing with this horrible institution of slavery. Maybe David had more ability to be discreet than he'd realized.

Enslaved.

Words rushed through Nathan's mind. *Unjust. Unfair. Abolition. Equality. Freedom. Underground Railroad.* Words Father had put into his vocabulary from Nathan's childhood on.

What was Nathan willing to do to help?

Chapter One

Burwell Plantation
Charles City, Virginia 1849

"Lettie!" The master's daughter, Phebe, had a voice that sounded like old Nanny Burwell's parrot squawking.

"Yes'm." Lettie stopped brushing the girl's long thick hair, so much like her own, and accidentally looked up into the mirror.

She caught her own breath before quickly averting her gaze. The image there seared into her mind like a branding iron. It was as though a younger Lettie was sitting on that fine mahogany chair in front of the vanity with a reflection of the older version standing behind her. Her hands trembled as she continued brushing Phebe's long tresses.

One enslaved sister serving, the other half-sister enjoying every benefit that their father could visit upon her. Lettie's whole body began to tremble.

Nathan Pleasant's words echoed in her soul. *"We need to get you out of here, Letitia."*

"Lettie! Pay attention. I asked if you had polished my new dancing shoes? If Mr. Pleasant shows up here today I'll demand that he shows me some new waltz steps. I've heard he's very good."

Was the girl reading her mind? No. But clearly Phebe believed Nathan had an interest in her. Was that perhaps the truth?

On every visit to Charles City, for his father's business, Nathan Pleasant made a stop at the Burwells' home. Nanny Burwell had insisted that since it was the closest plantation to Richmond and his last stop before returning home, that he always pay them a call before departing. Even the parrot had echoed Nanny's words on the last visit, "Come back!"

With each visit, Nathan had made sure he'd spoken with her. Twice, his friend Captain Bryant had arrived first and had Nanny send Lettie to the icehouse, where Nathan soon arrived. Her heart beat faster at the recollection of those stolen moments with him. He'd been kindness itself. Not at all like the master and his son and their cronies.

"Miss Phebe, those shoes shine brighter than a new copper kettle."

"A new copper kettle?" The girl scoffed. "What would I know of those?"

Lettie's cheeks heated. She'd begun life in the kitchen house where her mother was a kitchen slave. A new copper item was a sight to behold. Not to this girl, though. "Yes'm, you're right."

"Well bring them to me so I can see."

Lettie hurried to the corner and pulled the flannel dust covering from the shoes and brought them to their owner. To Lettie's owner, too, if truth be told. Owner and sister. This was one evil world.

"Open the curtains wider and lift the sash so we can get some fresh air in here."

Phebe's mother, if she wasn't in one of her laudanum-induced fogs, would shriek if she spied a window open in the house. But Lettie wasn't about to contradict Phebe. She'd earned

Love's Escape

too many slaps from the girl for daring to speak her mind. Now she kept her tongue firmly under control. "Yes'm."

Once she'd accomplished Phebe's bidding, Lettie looked out to the yard and beyond. A rider's horse kicked up dirt as the horse cantered toward the plantation. That was the captain. Would Nathan be shortly behind him? Lettie drew in a deep breath.

Escape. Freedom. Underground Railroad. God's provision. Faith. Help. Those were the words Nathan repeated on each visit, each time more firmly. *Watch, wait, be ready, someday soon, you can do this.* She chewed her lower lip. Those were all things that her mother insisted were impossible for the slaves on this plantation.

"Well what are you gawking at?" Phebe rose.

Lettie stepped aside and Phebe, standing only in her shift with her long hair down, stared out the window. "It's the captain!"

The girl whirled upon Lettie. "Don't just stand there get me ready."

Lettie ran to the wardrobe and opened it.

"No! Send Satilde up to help me and you go out and tell Mr. Bryant that I'll need a few moments to prepare to meet him."

How could the girl know if he came to see Phebe, her father, or even old Nanny Burwell? "Yes'm."

"Wait. I wondered something." Phebe's voice so cold and still reminded her of a water moccasin waiting to strike. "Have you noticed that Mr. Pleasant often follows his friend here?"

Lettie looked down at her scuffed boots. What should she say? Did the girl know of their visits?

"I'm not sure if he really and truly is calling upon Nanny or if he's really here to see me." The edge in the girl's voice could have sliced easily through wood.

He says he's here to see me. He says to be careful. He teaches me new things and tells me to watch. He says I must plan an escape. Lettie kept her thoughts to herself.

From the corner of her eye she saw Phebe wave her hand dismissively. "How would a stupid slave like you know? Just go and ask the good captain to be patient."

She wasn't stupid. She was learning new things. And if Nathan had his way, she'd one day no longer be a slave. "Yes'm." Lettie bobbed a curtsey and left the room.

Once outside the Big House, she ran across the courtyard and to the stables. Was Nathan on his way, too?

Was it possible that such a handsome and educated man might return the feelings that were growing in her? As much as she'd tried to quash them, in her dreams the dashing Mr. Pleasant rode in on a white horse, grabbed her up, and carried her away. Far away from the Burwells and the James River.

That niggling in her spirit, though, that warned her that Phebe Burwell suspected something—that nudged Lettie to ask a favor of Captain Bryant. A favor that would hurt like a whip stinging her back.

When she reached the stables, she pressed her hands to her stomach. She had to ask this. All of Mama's warnings agreed with this *knowing* she had.

Captain Bryant held the reins for his horse.

She curtsied. "I have a private message for you, sir."

"Oh?" He handed the reins to one of the slaves in the stable.

He joined her and the two of them walked a few steps down the brick pathway away from the building.

"I have a message from Miss Phebe that she's getting ready for you." She moistened her lips. "But also, sir, I need you to stop Mr. Pleasant from trying to visit me today. Is he coming?"

"Yes, he is, but why?"

Love's Escape

"I think Phebe maybe has figured this out."

She glanced up at the tall man, who scratched his chin.

"I could ride back to tell him, or I can make an excuse to wait for him out here."

Relief coursed through her. As much as she'd enjoy even a moment or two with Nathan, she couldn't risk endangering herself. Who knew what the Burwells might do to her or to Mama if they found out?

"I will walk down to their wharf and inspect their boats. That will earn me some time. And I'll watch for Nathan."

"And could you tell him something?"

"Anything."

"If I am never able to speak with him again I want him to know that I appreciate what he's done for me."

"Oh no. Don't even think for a moment that we won't try to get you out of here one way or another." The man's voice was so stern that Lettie flinched.

Don't give up. That small voice spoke to her heart.

Three months later
Burwell Plantation

Today, Nathan would put an end to Letitia's nonsense—her resistance to the notion of escaping—if he had to shackle her himself. His face burned at the uncharitable and wicked thought, not to mention the ridiculousness of wanting to force her to leave against her will. If not enslaved, the beautiful young woman wouldn't be in the predicament of trying to escape her plight. But she must be prudent.

At least David had begun to exercise more caution, His friend was becoming one of Father's most trusted conductors on the Underground Railroad. But he'd also learned how to manage

15

risk. If only Letitia could see that one must take chances for there to be freedom for her.

As he rode closer, Nathan scanned the fields of winter wheat as far as the eye could see. How did those slaves who simply ran without the benefit of a "conductor" manage?

They didn't.

Most of those escaped slaves were returned within a day. A shudder moved through him and coursed to his hands. He tugged at the reins, slowing his bay mare. Birdsong rose above the gentle *clip-clop* of his horse's hooves on the hard-packed road but did nothing to calm his taut nerves.

Ahead lay Burwell Plantation, its great house dominating the gentle hill.

A mockingbird imitated the shrill of a child's tin whistle.

Nathan pulled the reins to halt his mount and listened.

Letitia had been careful so far. She'd shared her desire to escape only with him. But what if she became desperate and loose lipped? What if she mistook an evildoer for a helper?

What if some *human mockingbird* imitated an Underground Railroad conductor? *Dear God, help her.*

Soon he'd arrived. One of the slaves, a tall slender man named Otheo, took care of Nathan's horse. "Thank you for your help."

Otheo cast him a brief dark gaze, averted his head, nodded, and then led the bay away.

Nathan huffed a sigh. Southern gentlemen didn't thank the slaves. The Williams family, at Dogwood Plantation, had been a great influence on Father as well as Nathan. Carter and Cornelia Williams had been among the first great abolitionists along the James River, before they'd moved North. The couple, in their sixties, were a key link on the Underground Railroad. Shivers moved down Nathan's arms as he strode along the brick path

Love's Escape

toward the Big House. That older couple had acted on their beliefs and so far the good Lord had protected them. May God grant Letitia safety if she found safe passage. If Nathan could find her a sure way out.

The doorman, an enslaved older man with silvery grizzled hair, dipped his chin. "You here for the master?"

"No, I'm here for Nanny Burwell. She should be expecting me."

The servant opened the door. Inside a gallery of Burwell ancestors gazed down at him in what he felt was disapproval. The boy inside the reception room took Nathan's riding jacket and hung it.

The parlor door opened, and tiny white-haired Mrs. Burwell ducked her head out. "We're in here, dear Nathan."

"Good to see you, Mrs. Burwell."

He went to the parlor and stepped inside. Letitia was seated at the window, stitching something. He straightened.

"You know Letitia, I believe." Nanny closed the parlor door and locked it.

Nathan's hands shook. What was afoot here?

"I don't want to be interrupted while I'm discussing my, er," Nanny waggled her eyebrows. "My options for my eventual departure for this earth. When we last visited, a few weeks ago, we were so rudely interrupted by my granddaughter, that I'm taking precautions."

He exhaled the breath he'd not realized had been pent up in his chest. So, she hadn't discovered that he and Letitia had secret meetings when he'd visited before.

He cast a quick glance at Letitia and she briefly met his gaze.

After Nathan and Nanny had exchanged more pleasantries and discussed the health of both families, Nathan explained in greater detail their funeral options.

"Well, of course you know I'll want the grandest that's ever been known in these parts." She gave him a sly grin. Nanny must have been quite the beauty in her day, with those sparkling green eyes that reminded him of someone else's.

"Let's have tea brought in. Lettie, would you do us the honors?" The widow spoke kindly, which had Nathan wondering yet again if she was onto the two of them.

Letitia departed.

"I'm an old woman, Nathan. I've lived a long life and I've had some regrets."

"You have a large and loving family, Nanny Burwell." Nathan hoped he sounded sincere. She had a large family who loved their wealth, status, and continued to hold people in bondage.

"My relations in England have been after me for some time to push my son to free our slaves. My own father was involved in the legislation to ban this institution in my home country. By then, I'd already married my husband and come here to live."

"I see." He wasn't sure if she was testing him.

"He'd been accustomed to slavery as a way of life and his father before him. I'm afraid that as a mother, I didn't do a very good job of helping my children see the error of their ways." A tear trickled down her wan cheek and she wiped it away.

Her husband had been an old tyrant.

"My husband didn't allow such talk and. . ." She waved her hand dismissively. "I'm sorry. That's all too late now."

Nathan pressed his lips together, unsure if he should speak.

"Young man, do what you can now to act on your beliefs and if you marry, please let your wife also have her say."

"Yes, ma'am."

"It may be too late for me, but you're young."

Love's Escape

The door opened and Letitia returned with the tea cart. Her hands shook as she poured tea for them and served them both oatmeal raisin cookies and ham biscuits.

"Mr. Pleasant, one reason I've chosen your father's funeral home for my send off, is because it is something that I can do. It's money well spent going to the right cause."

Nathan straightened. She knew. And if this elderly lady knew, then who else did?

Letitia's eyes widened.

Nanny Burwell pointed to the cart. "Lettie, leave that there and be a good girl and run out to the icehouse for me. I want some cream."

"Yes'm." Letitia bobbed a curtsey.

"And mind you, check every crock of cream for the one that's the coolest and the freshest, my dear." A conspiratorial smile tugged at the elderly lady's pink lips. "Each and every one and there are plenty."

"Yes'm. I'll take my time."

"That's right, you do that." She sipped her tea from her blue-and-white floral china tea cup.

Suddenly uncomfortable, Nathan shifted in his cushioned chair.

"Drink your tea and eat up because I'm sending you after her in a few minutes." Mrs. Burwell took a bite of a cookie.

What was she up to? Had she seen Nathan with Letitia before?

She must know.

"It's the only place you'll have privacy this afternoon for a few precious minutes."

Nathan stiffened. "What do you mean?"

"I've spent a long time on God's green earth and I've eyes in my head, unlike many of the others in this house. I don't trust many men, but I trust you, Nathan Pleasant. I fear for Lettie if she stays on this plantation much longer."

Was this a trick? Was this like the mockingbird earlier? Was she sincere?

"Ma'am, I'm not sure what you mean—"

She waved her hand dismissively. "Go to the icehouse and if anyone asks what you're doing there you explain it is for me."

"Yes, ma'am."

He rose.

Nanny Burwell sat there as calm as could be. If she was up to no good, she had an excellent poker face.

Nathan exited the parlor and the house and strode down the brick walkways on the Queen Anne court that mimicked that of Shirley Plantation, albeit on not quite so grand a scale.

Male slaves pushed wheelbarrows full of vegetables to the kitchen house. Other slaves, women, carried baskets piled high with linens and clothing from the laundry house toward the back of the Big House.

A breeze from the James River ruffled the leaves of the nearby dogwood trees. He continued on past the tall brick buildings until he reached the icehouse. He unlatched the door and entered, to the scent of the sawdust, which kept the ice from melting.

Letitia held a crock in her hands but set it down when he entered. He secured the door behind him.

"I want to get you out of here, Letitia." Nathan grasped Letitia's cold hands.

"It's not safe." She bit her lip. "You could get us both killed."

He gently squeezed her fingers. "The others have explained to me how to get you North—to freedom."

Love's Escape

"Lots of people get themselves on the way to freedom only to get captured." Letitia's green eyes widened. "And they come back to even worse horrors." She shuddered.

"That's true, but I could protect you." How, he wasn't sure, but he wanted to believe it. "We'd be together."

Letitia shook her head. "How do I know you're not taking me somewhere just to sell me into worse conditions—I've heard about men like that, too."

Nathan frowned. "Do you think that about me?"

She shrugged. "I don't know."

"We've been sneaking around like this for months." He'd brought her money today to keep in a safe place. "I'm getting more concerned about being found out here."

"Then stop coming." Lettie pouted. She knew she shouldn't. And what she'd just said was the furthest thing from what she wanted. But if Nathan could be deterred so easily then he certainly wasn't worth the risks he proposed. Even now, she had to keep constant vigilance when he came to the plantation.

"You know I can't. We've come so far. Your diction is perfect."

"I've been practicing when I'm alone." Both her reading and her writing, too.

"Good."

"Miss Phebe she watch me, she watches me, like a hawk."

"Do you think Phebe suspects something?" Nathan smelled good, like tea and oranges and spice not like the Burwell men and their guests, who often carried the odor of liquor and cigar smoke.

"Miss Burwell's not capable of thinking about much other than herself." She frowned. "But I do wonder."

Nathan exhaled loudly. "She strikes me as a jealous young woman."

21

Lettie couldn't help but laugh. "She makes accusations and acts jealous because she's cavorting about with a half-dozen young bucks in the county."

"So that's part of her game?"

"She says she has to make all her beaus think she's jealous if they flirt with anyone else."

"You and I have never flirted, have we?"

Lettie stiffened. Yet something else she'd never have, as an enslaved woman. "Maybe you call your speaking with me about your faith as flirting, do you?"

"No." He took a step back from her. "That was genuine conversation and concern."

"You are a serious young man." The other interactions she'd had with white men, in general, had been terse at best and frightening at worst.

"Listen, I think we have a friend in Nanny Burwell."

She drew in a slow, deep breath. "I've wondered the same, from how she treat, how she treats me, and what she's said."

"I'm of the opinion that she could help us. Possibly only financially, but perhaps in other ways."

"She's been giving me old clothing of the girls'. She's asked me to mend and wash it. When I asked about giving it back, she said I should start wearing it more and that she'd tell the master she wanted me looking nice in the house."

A line formed between Nathan's eyes. "That sounds promising, but do be careful."

She shivered.

"It's cold in here." Nathan bent his head, a lock of hair falling across his brow. "Listen, remember what I told you about watching for an opportunity while I work with David on a plan. I have to get you out of here."

She raised her eyebrows. "You didn't listen to me. I said I'm scared."

Too scared to run. And what might that cost her?

Chapter Two

Richmond, Spring 1850

How could love feel like this? Now Nathan was imagining things that could not be. A faint mist cloaked the city. The woman's large hat may have deceived his eyes into seeing what he wished.

The young woman he'd visited secretly for nigh on two years, would never have been allowed to travel to Richmond and to linger in the street in front of the dressmaker's shop. Had she escaped? Had the tools he'd given her—the ability to read, the encouragement to copy the speech patterns of her captors, and the money to be used only if she had a confirmed method to safely leave—given her the courage to flee to freedom?

He hurried toward the auburn-haired woman, adjusting his waistcoat as he strode forward. She clutched her hands at her waist. The woman's defeated stance and the stiffness in her shoulders declared this had to be his Letitia. She stared straight ahead.

Nathan slowed his steps. It was too good to be true.

Like his friend, David, he'd given the woman he'd come to love the means to grab her freedom if it became available. They'd both worked on an escape plan, but when David's beloved had been taken to England, and planned to remain behind there, where

Love's Escape

slavery was prohibited, his friend had withdrawn his offer to bring Nathan and Letitia North.

He'd grabbed every opportunity his father had given him to make trips to Charles City. And when he did, he'd always stopped at Burwell Plantation, to try to sneak in some conversation with the woman he longed to help break free.

The lady near the dressmaker's shop lifted her head.

His heart leapt. "Letitia," he whispered.

She cast a quick glance toward the open door of the shop. Nathan followed her gaze. Inside, the elderly Nanny Burwell spoke with the proprietress. She held her pince-nez up, the eyeglasses black velvet ribbon dangling, as she bent over a bolt of a blue patterned fabric.

He couldn't help but smile. Nanny Burwell, who kept calling him out to the plantation, and giving him more and more sums for her funeral, had already funded trips on the Underground Railroad for some dozen escaped slaves. Not that the woman was told so.

He drew nearer. "What are you doing here?" Delight shot through him, both at her presence and at the notion that she'd finally made it off the Burwell property. That was a start. The first step of what he hoped would be a long journey far away from Virginia.

"Old Mrs. Burwell insisted to the master that I come with her on this trip." Letitia jumped as a coach drove by in the street. "And she wouldn't take no for an answer. Left without his say so."

Nathan took her hands, but she pulled them free. A stranger, attired in workman's garb, strode by and cast an admiring glance at Letitia. Jealousy reared up in him. "But what are you doing out here?"

She bit her lower lip. "That driver of hers, he high-tailed it over to the Swan Tavern." She pointed across the busy street.

"And I'm trying to keep an eye out for him. He was supposed to remain with the carriage."

The Burwell's distinctive carriage was parked nearby along the roadway. "No footman?"

"No. Mr. Burwell said he couldn't spare him today, and our driver was supposed to help us. But he's gone off."

"I couldn't believe it when I saw you." Were they really out in society standing together on the street?

What would it be like if they could be together without looking over their shoulders?

What would it be like if she could simply be with Nathan, in free society? But standing here, on the boardwalk, Letitia felt as though every eye was on her. That everyone passing by knew she was a slave. That they were secretly mocking her.

"Letitia?" Nathan peered down at her, with a concerned expression on his handsome face.

"I was just thinking…"

"Well, instead of thinking, I want you to grab this opportunity."

"To escape?" She raised her eyebrows.

"Not unless you have a clear and safe plan."

"No. I feel scared just being away from the plantation. How am I gonna act like a real lady if you and Captain Bryant get me out?"

Nathan inhaled loudly. "For today, do this for me—act as though you really and truly are a free woman. You're not a slave. You're a working woman, here as a seamstress, to look for extra work."

"I'll try." When she got back, she'd not even be able to tell Mama about all the feelings she had.

"Straight back. Chin up."

She stood taller. Two matrons passing them cast a quizzical glance at her. "It'd be easier if I could dress the part."

"Could you convince Nanny to give you some more hand-me-downs that you could make over in case we can get you out?"

"I ... I think so." If she could be given some fancy lace and embellishments that would be even better.

"And would you pray with me that I can come up with something that would work? A way to get you out that is the safest of all?"

"Yes, I will."

Nathan shook his head. "I'm going over to the Swan to check on your driver. I'll not have a drunkard driving you and Mrs. Burwell home."

Letitia dipped her chin in acknowledgement.

Nathan waited for two riders, atop a pair of magnificent, matched bays, pass by. Then he and several others crossed the street.

Once inside the tavern, he immediately recognized the Burwells' driver—a tall, thin man with stringy gray hair tied back in an old-style queue. He and several other similar-looking men sat at a round oak table, empty tankards covering the entire tabletop. From the man's bloodshot eyes and his loud cackling laugh, it was clear he was well into his cups.

And not fit to drive.

What had he told Letitia repeatedly? *Use every opportunity.*

Nathan exited the building and ran across the street, which was clear. He nodded to Letitia. "He's drunk and I'll not have him bringing you two ladies home."

Letitia's face paled. "What will we do?"

"Leave it to me."

He entered the dressmaker's shop and tipped his hat at the handful of ladies inside.

Nanny Burwell spied him and smiled. "Why young Mr. Pleasant, what brings you here? Finally found yourself a wife?" She laughed.

He certainly hoped he had. But that might never be. "Your driver has been heavily drinking over at the Swan Tavern and I've come to offer my assistance."

Her thin white eyebrows drew together. "Oh my. Can your father spare you?"

He bent at the waist. "Of course, ma'am. I am at your service."

"You ought to leave him at the tavern and let him find his own way back to Charles City." The shop owner wagged her index finger. "That would teach him."

"Yes. I'll do just that." Mrs. Burwell pulled at her ecru lace collar. Her old-fashioned garb was more reminiscent of two decades or more earlier. "I'm getting my funeral dress made up. It's a deep purple shade."

"Oh."

She pointed to a bolt of eggplant color moiré satin. "It's beautiful. From France."

"I have that same shade in my new coat and matching pants, with a mustard stripe." David had mocked Nathan for his choice, but he thought it to be quite fashionable.

"Well then, you must be the one who stands beside me at my wake."

"Absolutely." He did enjoy the older woman's cheeky comments.

"But until I drop dead, why don't you bring the carriage around and take me and young Lettie home?" A sly grin stole over her pale face.

"I can have my errand boy run a message to your father, if you wish." The shop owner pointed to a dark-skinned lad not much more than ten.

Nathan recognized the freedman's son. "Yes, please tell my father that I'll find a way back."

"Nonsense." Nanny shook her head, which caused her white curls to bounce. "We'll have another driver bring you back—one who's not intoxicated."

"Thank you." Nathan tossed a coin to the boy, who caught it with both hands, eyes wide.

Mrs. Burwell completed her purchases and Nathan took her elbow and brought her outside and down the steps as a shop assistant carried the wrapped purchases outside.

"Lettie, this young man is going to drive us back."

"Yes'm." Lettie accepted the packages from the shop girl, averting her eyes.

He assisted Nanny up into the carriage.

She cast him a strange look. "The next time you drive me could be for my burial."

"Mrs. Burwell—"

She waved him away as she settled in on the black leather bench seat. "All my loved ones have been coming to visit me. It could be any time now. Help your father make something big enough and grand enough for me."

He nodded.

She winked at him. "Why, I'd like a coffin big enough that both Lettie and I could fit in it." She gave him a meaningful glance.

Nathan turned and took the packages from Letitia. Before he could assist her up, she'd already gotten into the carriage. He placed the packages on the seat beside Letitia.

"I've driven many a carriage and dray, so have no fear, ladies." He'd included Letitia, something he shouldn't have done. His neck heated.

"While you're driving you think about what I said, young man. I'm sure Lettie wouldn't mind coming with me when I go." She raised her eyebrows.

Letitia looked shocked.

"Yes, ma'am."

Soon they were on their way. He mulled over the older woman's words. Something niggled at him in his spirit. Nanny was almost as eccentric as his father was, and she had a bit of the bluestocking left in her—but surely she wasn't referring to how in some cultures servants and animals would be buried alive with their masters. No. There was another meaning. Surely.

And as the wind swirled around him, inside his thoughts danced and created a vessel that could carry not one person from this world to another, but two. And if it worked, how could he convince volunteers to travel in such an unusual manner?

When they arrived, he assisted Nanny Burwell out. "There you go, ma'am."

She smiled up at him. "Did you think about what I said?"

"Mrs. Burwell, if you had the most magnificent casket amongst all the plantation families you know the rest would want them, too."

"Exactly!" Her eyes brightened as she tapped his shoulder.

Exactly. And if the plantation owners all wanted the elaborate coffin, then more travelers could slip out with them to Richmond.

As he helped Letitia down, a plan and a hope hatched.

Room for two.

Charles City, Virginia

Love's Escape

As he neared the plantation buildings, a groom ran up from the stable. After he handed off his mare, Nathan strode across the green to the big house. Today he'd tell Letitia his plan and urge her to do nothing to alter her circumstances until he could set everything in place. Would she trust him?

The scent of woodsmoke, ham, and spicy apples wafted from the kitchen house as he passed.

"Lettie! You gets back in here now, girl!"

Stiffening, Nathan turned to face the two-story brick building to his right. A slender, light-skinned servant stood framed in the entryway, her head covered by a bright cloth, her shabby dress too short over her bare feet. She met his eyes.

"Letitia?" His voice was barely a whisper, and she couldn't have heard him, for a plump, dark-skinned woman jerked her arm and pulled her back into the kitchen.

What was Lettie doing in the kitchen house? And why wasn't she wearing attire suitable for her position as a house servant?

Sweat broke out on his brow. Visitors weren't normally allowed near the kitchen house. How would he speak with her?

"Mister Pleasant!" Burwell's eldest daughter, Phebe, bedecked in a blue-and-purple-striped gown, stood on the front porch, twirling a parasol over her dark head—unnecessary since she was in the shade of the portico's overhang.

When he joined her, Miss Burwell linked her arm through his and ushered Nathan inside. "Papa will be so glad to see you. Wants to thank you properly for bringing Nanny home, and that slave girl, too."

"No trouble at all." At least for him. But had the Burwell women sensed something between him and Letitia? "Is your house servant now moved to the kitchen?"

Phebe cast a sidelong look at him. "We'd had enough of Lettie's uppity ways."

Nathan stiffened and averted his gaze, not wanting her to see his anger. Surely Letitia hadn't been practicing his remonstration of chin up and shoulders back while she was working in the house. No. He'd observed her. More likely it was Phebe's jealousy provoking this reaction. Still, had his advice now placed Letitia in a precarious position?

"Now Mr. Pleasant, why don't you tell me why you're *really* here?" Her coy voice irritated, yet never had he been so grateful for the vixen's misconstrued notion that he held an interest in her. But her jealousy of Letitia now put the one who he truly sought almost out of his reach. "A gentleman doesn't play all his cards at once, Miss Burwell."

Laughing, she twirled her parasol. "Why, Mr. Pleasant, does this mean you finally intend to ask Papa if you may court me?"

If it got him out there again and close to Letitia, he'd do it. But his gut rebelled.

When he didn't respond, she tilted her head back and laughed. "You'll have to fight David Bryant for that chance."

His shock must have shown on his face because she giggled. His closest friend had never mentioned an interest in Phebe and had his own plans. "Will Captain Bryant be bringing you out our way when he comes back into port?"

What game was Phebe playing?

Perspiration broke out on his collar.

Lettie was in grave danger. He could feel it in his bones.

Chapter Three

Burwell Plantation
Charles City, Virginia

How dare the stars still light the night and the James River continue to flow, when the one who made Lettie's life bearable was gone? *Oh, Mama.*

Lettie wailed again, catching her tears with her dirty apron. She sank down onto the oak bench, shoved against the plastered wall. The cool, rough surface nudged through the thin cotton of her work shirt, but she didn't care. How much pain had her mother endured before she'd finally fainted? And then died, within hours.

Lettie trembled and fisted her hands. Revenge should be hers—not the Lord's. Hurt, fury, and disgust swirled into a violent brew powerful enough to blow everyone up on this plantation.

A candle flickered as a slender figure descended the kitchen-house brick stairs. "You all right, Lettie?" Her friend Nestor extended a dark hand, and Lettie clasped it.

"No, I'm not fine at all." Wouldn't ever be again. Lettie hiccupped a sob.

Her beautiful mother was gone. But what good had her beauty brought? Her mother was far prettier than their mistress, and that had resulted in Mama being kept in the kitchen and never allowed inside the house. Lettie had been proclaimed better-looking than the Burwell daughters, who continually sought to insult her or get her in trouble.

But it was their wicked overseer who'd brought about her mother's downfall, despite the master being the one who had allowed the whipping. Wasn't God like that? *He'd let this happen.* What kind of Savior was that who'd let such evil persist?

The fellow slave girl sat down beside her. "It ain't right what they done. You knows it, and I do, too."

"No. It was pure evil." A knot had formed in her throat, and she choked with emotion.

Nestor set the candlestick down and pulled her into a shivering embrace. "What you gonna do, Lettie? About that overseer?"

She shook her head. If she could, she'd kill Durham in his sleep. But with Satilde likely sleeping right in there with him, she daren't try.

"You think Satilde mean what she say?"

Satilde was the overseer's favorite slave and his mistress. Which had given the young woman powerful sway over him—except when it came to other slaves he wanted to subject to his perverted desires. Only Mama and Satilde's influence had stood between Durham forcing Lettie to come to his cabin once she'd been moved out of the Big House. Before then, she'd been protected.

He'd never have dared grab her in the Big House.

"I don't know." Lettie sniffed and wiped at her eyes. "With Mama gone. . ."

"Satilde was right about what nasty ol' Durham would do first." Nestor's eyes widened. "She say he gonna get your mama out of the way. Then he get what he wants."

Lettie sucked in a hard breath and held it, before releasing a slow exhale, willing herself to chase away the terror that Satilde's

Love's Escape

words had brought her. "But Master Burwell allowed it." She stifled a sob. Worse yet, why had this powerful God she worshipped let her mother be murdered?

"I hear it was the missus who give Durham permission."

"No. That's not true." Lettie had been delivering a pot of tea to the master's office and was in the hidden alcove outside when the overseer had stomped in, bellowing about her mother and her supposed defiance. "Mrs. Burwell on too much laudanum to complain about much."

Lettie should have done something. She should have gone in and contradicted Durham. Should have. . .

Nestor's eyes filled. "Well, you gonna die, then, girl, just like your mama done, 'cause I know you ain't givin' yourself to that piece of trash."

A long shudder coursed through Lettie. She was going to die. Just like her mother had. Lettie would refuse him. Would keep away from him. Then he'd concoct a story about her, lie to the master, and that would be the end of her, too. She shuddered out a sob.

"Girl, don't even think about givin' yourself to him, 'cause Satilde already say she gonna stick a knife in your heart if you lie with her man."

Lettie dug a rag from her apron pocket and blew her nose. This had been the only home she'd ever known. The kitchen house stood northeast of the Big House. The brick kitchen building, with its two stories, would be a beautiful home if she were free. But Letitia wasn't. She was Mr. Burwell's slave. As had been her mother.

But Parkes was Mama's surname, taken from old Mr. Parkes who'd first owned her—not that slaves were allowed to use a second name. The only reason her mother hadn't been tossed in the ground like dirt was because of Mr. Parkes. The old man sent his boy over to tell the Burwells that he demanded that Mama be buried on his property.

"I hear Mr. Pleasant gonna put your mama in a fine box. Um hmm."

"Mr. Pleasant?" Hope nudged its blossom upward, pushing aside her soul's hardened soil. She might have one day, or maybe two, before Durham would come looking for her, if she was lucky.

When Nathan Pleasant heard of her plight, would he make his offer again? Would he come for her as he'd promised?

"That's what I heard. Ol' Mr. Parkes, he gonna pay for one of the Pleasants' finest coffins in Richmond. One good enough even for Nanny."

Nanny had been so good to her. Once, she'd cried a little and said if she could die and Nathan could take her and Lettie away, that she'd do it. But it would be a sin to take her own life. Lettie worried that Nanny was losing her wits. But Nathan had said Nanny had given them a good plan.

Her heartbeat skipped and jumped. "Nestor, make me a promise."

"What?"

Lettie pressed a hand to her chest. "When Mr. Pleasant arrives, come and get me no matter where I am."

Nestor nibbled her full lower lip. "I do my best, but there's a new girl comin' tomorrow, too, I heard."

"Oh? They're replacing Mama already?" Lettie frowned.

"The Dolleys' town girl—whose fancy owners treated her like she their own child." Her friend made a sound of disgust.

"Not Beneida?"

"That be her name."

Beneida was Nathan's friend, David's sweetheart—though Lettie was scolded to never disclose that fact.

"But she was supposed to be freed." Nathan said Beneida planned to get free in England, when her owners were there. But the Dolley family had recently returned with her in tow. "Her owner just died. Mr. Dolley said in his will—"

"It don' matter what he put in there—only matters what be decided by his wife. And Mrs. Dolley say Beneida be sold to Master Burwell."

"What?"

"I think Mrs. Dolley secretly jealous of that girl."

"Yes." Beneida believed so, too, from what Nathan had said. What heartache the young woman must be suffering. And what danger Beneida would encounter with Durham once he caught sight of the young woman who David claimed outshone all the beautiful belles in Virginia.

She and Beneida had to get out of here. Could the persistent Mr. Pleasant be true to his word and help them leave?

Lord, you've allowed the worst—Mama is gone—don't disappoint me now.

༺❀༻

Pleasant Funerary
Richmond, Virginia

Nathan paced the outer corridor's stone floors, eyeing the scuff marks of the many who'd lived, and died, over the years. *White people.*

But in the back—that was a different matter. Not one of their white patrons suspected that an Underground Railroad link stood right under this roof.

More slaves would be freed soon, if their new coffin design worked. His brother, Jules, and he would be convincing some wealthy Virginians to purchase a much more elaborate coffin, one that possessed a secret compartment.

The interior door to the blue-and-gold wallpapered viewing room opened, and his father slipped out. At sixty-five, Martin Pleasant's face glowed with good health. Father clapped Nathan's shoulder. "Have you set up the viewings for the Alderman family?"

"Yes, sir. All taken care of. They were very kind and appreciative of all you have set up for them."

"Good." Father stroked his clean-shaven chin, beneath his heavy white muttonchops. "And you'll be going out to Burwell's plantation in the morning?"

"Yes, sir." His heartbeat accelerated. He must see Letitia again while he was there. But he had to be very careful.

The Burwell Plantation, not far from Richmond, was home to the woman who'd turned his life upside down. From the first time he'd met her, his thoughts kept returning to Letitia. She could easily be mistaken as one of the master's daughters. Never had he laid eyes on so beautiful a creature, with a lovely heart-shaped face. When he'd been informed the angelic girl was, in fact, a slave, his notions of what his life would be altered to one of complete change. All of his father's words over the years, about abolitionism, ceased being something for others to be involved with. Now Nathan's eyes had been opened. His heart was no longer his own. And the one he loved was in bondage.

Behind them, one of the entry doors opened.

Father's quickly affixed "funeral home" face slipped off, and he quirked an eyebrow. "David. Welcome."

Nathan turned to find David Bryant, hatless, his dark hair shooting in a dozen different directions, his ascot askew. "Have you a moment for a friend?"

Father gave a quick nod of approval and headed off toward the office.

Love's Escape

"Are you unwell, David?" Nathan gestured for his friend to go into the casket room.

"No." The captain's voice was hoarse. "Beneida has been sold."

"What?" Nathan's hushed voice flew out as a hiss. "But she was to be freed." And she and David were to run off together; if his friend had his wish.

A heavy weight settled in Nathan's chest as he opened the walnut-paneled door and stepped into the very room where Beneida's mistress had just that morning selected a casket for her husband.

He closed the door behind him. "What happened? Where is she going?"

"She's been sent to Burwell's."

"No. Oh, Lord, be merciful." He knew what a hard taskmaster Burwell was and that his overseer was notorious for brutality. Nathan pressed his eyelids closed. Rebellious notions of rescuing Letitia, fed by seeds of David's discontent and plans to one day begin a new life with Beneida, had blossomed in Nathan months earlier. But Letitia had rejected his plan as being too dangerous. He'd vowed that the next time he saw her he'd disclose his family's part as conductors in the Underground Railroad.

"I believe the Lord is telling me to act, Nathan."

He met his friend's dark eyes. "What are you thinking?" He and Father had discussed a plan to get David's sweetheart onto a ship, but then Beneida had gone to England with the Dolleys, and they'd shelved the notion.

"I want to go out to Burwells and buy her contract."

Nathan couldn't stop the curt laugh that burst out of him. "You know Burwell would never do that. What is *his* is always his."

a relationship between the two of them. David, edging up on thirty, had waited all these years for Beneida to be freed.

With only room for a single soul to escape, must one couple's happiness and freedom be forever sacrificed?

Chapter Four

The stench of slave broker Hiram Cheney's tobacco, sweat, and alcohol was only intensified by his heavy use of bergamot oil. Lettie held her breath as she backed away from the open entryway, through which the paunchy man was shoving Beneida, the Dolleys' servant. Lettie released a gasp. She'd met the beautiful young slave several times—the first time when Lettie accompanied old Mrs. Burwell to see her dressmaker in Richmond.

Today Beneida wore a pink-and-yellow-checked day dress that was as fine as any Virginia society belle's. Lettie pressed a hand to her throat. She couldn't voice her question: What was Beneida doing in their kitchen?

"Where's Burwell?" The irksome man pulled a heavy watch from his purple-and-sky-blue plaid vest.

Lettie backed up into the kitchen window and startled when her apron strings tapped against the glass.

Nestor dipped a little curtsey and ducked her head. "He where he usually be, Mr. Cheney. Up in the big house."

The man grinned; his pockmarked ruddy face one Lettie had encountered in her nightmares. The other slaves told stories of this man as though speaking of the devil himself. No one wanted to be taken from Burwell Plantation by Cheney and sold elsewhere. Who knew what all he would do before they ever reached their destination?

"Why, lookie here." He chucked Nestor under her chin. "Things has worked out fine for ya here, ain't they?"

"Yes, sir."

Lettie must have been staring, for Cheney growled as he looked at her. She quickly glanced away and moved from the window to the stove.

"I'd say I was sorry about your mama, Lettie, but I ain't a man to lie." He patted the pockets of his burgundy coat.

She chewed her lip, willing the tears to stay put.

"Fact is, I was surprised it ain't happened earlier."

"Mr. Cheney, you want to try my new sugar biscuits?" Nestor's voice was tight as her eyes flashed briefly to Lettie and back to the disgusting man.

The man clomped across the brick floor with his filthy boots. "Why, if I had more time, I'd gladly savor some of your sugar biscuits, Nestor."

Lettie cringed at the insinuation in the insufferable man's voice.

Beneida sniffled in the corner.

"But I got to hand off this handsome gal and git on back to Richmond afore the boat departs. Got me a hundred. . ."—he used a derogatory term that set Lettie's teeth on edge—"to take down to Charleston."

Lettie turned to cast a sideways glance at the man, who was touching Beneida in an all-too-familiar manner. "Just remember your place and don't be puttin' on no fancy airs here, girl, and Miz Burwell might keep you."

As beautiful as the young woman was, who knew what shame Beneida would know at this plantation? Or had already suffered at Cheney's hands. Mama had somehow been able to keep the young Burwell men from her and had prevented Durham from getting near her, but now. . . Tears flowed down her cheeks, and she bent to stir the stew simmering on the hearth.

"Goin' up to the fields. Burwell weren't at the house when I stopped." Cheney spit a glob of tobacco onto their clean kitchen floor. "Wipe that up, girl."

He pushed Beneida toward the filth. When she hesitated, he kicked her. "Use that fancy gown of yours. Ya won't be wearin' it here."

Beneida grabbed a handful of the taffeta fabric but found what Lettie knew—the stiff fabric wouldn't pick it up—it merely smeared the foul substance around.

Spinning on his heel, Cheney cackled as he heavy-footed it out of the kitchen.

Lettie whooshed out a breath. She grabbed a wet rag and brought it over to wipe up the tobacco clump.

Nestor offered their newcomer a hand up. "You be Beneida?"

"Yes."

Lettie bent and wiped up the dark stain. If only life's messes were that easy to clean up. If only God could blot out the sins of men and restore them to right reasoning. Would they realize enslaving people was wrong?

"I heard about you." Nestor plucked at her shabby gray cotton skirt, beneath her stained apron.

"How so?" Beneida nibbled her lower lip.

"Lettie here say you gonna be free. That you go to England."

Her oval face paled. "I did. But we returned. Mr. Dolley died. And his wife sold me to the Burwells." Tears streamed down her face, and little Nestor patted her arm.

Beneida stared out through the windows. "I've never lived anywhere but in town."

Lettie followed her gaze. Outside, well-muscled field slaves pushed carts of produce to the back of the kitchen house. A number of men sat on the ground by the well, drinking their fill of water before they headed back. Across the yard, female slaves carried baskets of laundry atop their heads and into the laundry building. Smoke curled up where huge pots of water boiled for the task.

Chauncey Burwell rode up the center lawn astride his white gelding, waving his hat high. He circled the square, and the kitchen workers all quickly turned their attention to chopping vegetables on the counter. Even Beneida picked up a knife, in pretense.

"You look ridiculous in that outfit in here." Lettie shook her head.

"Everything I brought in my bundle is this fancy or more so." Beneida gingerly fingered the glossy bow on her right shoulder.

"I've got extra clothing upstairs you can use."

"She got more problems than clothing if she stay here." Nestor pointed toward the overseer, who was ducking into the laundry building—where he had no business to be.

Sweat rolled down Nathan's neck into his ivory linen cravat as he brought the Pleasant Funerary's conveyance to a halt midway up the Burwells' circular drive. "You go up to the house and distract them while I speak with Letitia and explain our plan."

A muscle in David's cheek jumped. He looked as nervous as Nathan felt. "All right."

Slipping from the wagon, Nathan jogged up the stairs of the kitchen house. To the right, several women chopped vegetables. Letitia bent over a board, her face wan and tear-streaked.

The sting of onions pricked his eyes. But it didn't account for the lump forming in his throat *That must be why my eyes are misting.*

The beautiful woman looked up and gasped. "Nathan?"

He coughed. "Can I get a cup of water?"

She wiped her hands on her apron and grabbed a tin cup and headed toward him. What would it be like to grab her up into his arms and carry her off? Wasn't that what he was about to do?

A dark-haired woman, attired in a dress more suited for the drawing room, swiveled to face him. "Mr. Pleasant!"

"Good day, Miss Dolley." How strange to act as though all was normal. As though they were in town, and he'd passed her in the street.

Lettie joined him and pressed the cup of water into his hands, their fingers touching briefly. She looked up at him, pleading in her eyes. How he longed to comfort her. She broke the connection and turned to face a short servant standing behind her.

"Nestor, would you please finish your chopping out back for a moment?"

The younger woman scooped up her bowl, a knife, and a small board and passed them, eyes downcast.

"I trust her, but we need privacy, don't we?" Lettie's breathy words stabbed his heart.

"Indeed."

"Oh, Nathan, I'm not safe here."

"I know, that's why we're here."

Beneida stopped chopping. "Is David here?"

"He's at the big house right now."

"Oh!" She pressed a hand to her mouth.

Taking Lettie's hand, Nathan led her out to the passageway between the two large rooms on the building's first floor. He'd already closed the front entryway door on his way in, so they were less likely to be seen.

"Thank God you're here, Nathan. Praise be to God." Tears rolled down her cheeks.

"I know about your mother." He took her hands and rubbed his thumb over her knuckles.

"But do you know who and why?" The pain in her eyes made him long to soothe it away.

"We heard rumors."

Letitia's thin cotton dress shook in ripples as she trembled. "The overseer is straight from the devil."

If he could, Nathan would pummel the man. But such would not be tolerated. "We have to get you out of here."

He was right. He'd been right all along.

"We don't have a lot of time, so listen." His clipped tone made her stiffen.

"All right."

"Mr. Parkes has paid for your mother to have a special casket and to be transported to his plantation for burial."

"No wonder, then, that they put her there"—Lettie's lower lip quivered—"in the icehouse."

"But you're coming with us."

"How?"

Someone in the next room sang a spiritual in a low voice.

"You'll accompany me to get your mother's body."

She nodded. Chopping noises in the adjacent preparation room made her flinch.

"Then you'll slip into the back of the wagon."

"All right."

"Then you'll climb into the bottom of the casket."

"What?" she lifted her head and stared wide-eyed at him.

"Shh!" Nathan squeezed her hands. "Do what I say, and all will be well."

"Lord Almighty knows I'm gonna die here if I don't do somethin' quick." Letitia released his hands and swiped at her tears.

"We're trying to get Beneida out soon, too."

"If you take me, you gotta take her, too, or that overseer will have her, he will."

How Nathan longed to hold Letitia, to assure her. "We have to see what we can do."

The front door to the building opened and a young slave carried in a basket of kitchen rags and towels.

Letitia accepted the willow basket from her. "Thank you."

Without a glance at Nathan, the servant turned and departed, leaving the door open to the cool river breezes.

Wagon wheels rolling over the crushed oyster shell drive sounded outside.

A fine glossy coach stopped in front of the kitchen. Letitia took several steps, her thin shoes' soles shuffling over the brick floor. She leaned out of the door frame then returned to his side.

"It's Master Parkes, my Mama's father, if rumors be true." She nibbled on her lower lip, as if resisting saying more.

No wonder the man had requested Letitia's mother's body, which would otherwise have been ignominiously thrown in the ground by the Burwells. "Thank God for his mercy."

"What?" Letitia blinked at him.

This wasn't the time to get into conversations about masters sleeping with their servants. But blast the man. Parkes could disrupt their entire plan.

"Let me go out to him." As he turned, Nathan spied David exiting the house, frowning. Nathan gestured for David to join

49

him as Letitia scurried off to the kitchen. David jogged across the lawn.

"Nanny wished us the best." David drew in a deep breath. "And her parrot—you won't believe this—for the first time that bird squawked at me to not come back."

The Lord worked in mysterious ways. Who was to say that even a parrot couldn't be used to convey a message? "So we have no invitation to return."

"We won't need it, my friend." His friend's dark eyebrows drew together. "Plan B. We need to get Beneida out of here, too, from what Nanny said."

"God knows what we need. And we need Him now more than ever."

From the kitchen, Lettie eyed the Pleasants' hearse wagon. They'd have to take it to the icehouse for Mama's body. She let the tears run down her face then wiped them with the back of her hand. A hand as pale as any of the Burwells'. And now she knew why she'd resembled them so much. Which made her blood father's betrayal all the more cutting. He'd allowed Mama to be whipped to death to put an end to his wife's nagging that she didn't want her or her daughter there on the property. Could she blame Mrs. Burwell for not wanting to accept her husband's behavior and the result of his sin—her, Lettie?

But she had to get Beneida out, too. How could she do it? That girl wouldn't last at Burwell Plantation for more than a few days. Too beautiful for the big house, too incompetent for the kitchen, how would the woman—who should have been freed—last in the fields? How long before Durham made her his next target?

Lettie moved into the opening to the preparation room, which now held a dozen slaves preparing for the midday meal, hoping to catch Beneida's eye. With her mother now gone, and no one really in charge yet, Lettie clasped her hands at her waist, as Mama had done, and stood, shoulders squared. "You come on with me now, Beneida. I got work for you elsewhere."

The others quickly raised their eyes in disbelief but resumed their efforts when Lettie gave them a curt nod.

The newcomer dragged her knife across the chopping board, pushing cut carrots into a large blue bowl, then set the bowl atop the table, wiped her hands on her apron, and joined Lettie.

Turning, Lettie led the woman upstairs to their rooms. "If you have anything at all you need to take with you, stow it on your person now."

"Why?"

"We leave soon." Heart hammering, Lettie pushed open the rickety door to her room. It squeaked in protest. She was lucky to have a door.

Beneida hauled up a canvas bag from beside her pallet.

"You can't take all that. It won't fit in a casket, I'm guessing."

"What?" The other woman's squeaky voice grated on Lettie.

"I'm already shaking in these here house shoes, so don't make things worse."

Beneida bobbed her dark head and pulled a few things from the bag. "Where are we going?"

"Don't know." Lettie scanned the room, dizziness threatening. *Be strong.*

She had nothing of value. She examined the window's ledge where a string of the Burwell girls' cast-offs trailed. Once she'd thought the silvery button, the piece of yellow ribbon, the bit of lace, the satin rosebud all treasures. *Not now.*

David pressed the silver flask into her trembling hands and Beneida gulped greedily, eyes closed, before handing it back and wiping her mouth.

"Get in." David did sound like a captain, with that commanding voice.

Beneida climbed up on the back of the wagon and then crawled into the bottom of the casket. Nathan joined David and lowered the top section.

The two men set about transferring the chill, blanket-covered form of Burwell's deceased cook from where she'd been laid in the icehouse. In death, her face was serene, reflecting a peace she'd likely never known in this life. How could God allow this travesty to continue?

How can man allow the sin of slavery?

The two men carried the body to the wagon, set it gently into the top portion of the box, and then closed the casket.

Letitia stood, arms clasped across her bosom, trembling from head to foot. She stared at them, as though unseeing.

"We must go." Nathan pointed inside.

When she made no move to join them, Nathan jumped down from the wagon, heart pounding. They had to get out of here before anyone noticed the two women had not returned to the kitchen.

"You have to get in."

Letitia shook her head.

"You must jump up in the back."

"No, she doesn't." A commanding, but tremoring, voice sliced the chill air.

Heart sticking in his chest, Nathan whirled around.

Chapter Five

Lettie bit back a cry as silver-haired Rushworth Parkes stabbed his cane into the hard-packed dirt floor strewn with straw and then lurched forward toward them. As he neared, he pointed to her. "My eyes were once as green as yours."

Lettie returned her gaze to the ground, hadn't realized she'd been staring at the man who was purported to be her grandpappy. But she'd taken in his frail appearance quickly: large feet like both Mama and she had, large hands like Mama's, and tall if he could straighten.

The man shuffled nearer, as both Nathan and Mr. Bryant closed the casket. Beneida's soft sobs carried out.

Mr. Bryant tapped the side. "Hush now, Beneida."

Dry, paperlike skin covered the fingers that lifted Lettie's chin. "You're so beautiful—the image of my mother."

No wonder Lettie had never been allowed in the house when the Parkes family had visited. She'd relished those times when she and Mama had stayed upstairs in the kitchen house, out of view.

The elderly man's eyes were filmed over with age. "Even with my bad eyes, I can see your hair is the exact shade of auburn mine once was." He fingered a stray curl by her ear.

Nathan jumped from the wagon and joined them. "We best get going Mr. Parkes."

This man, her grandpappy, extended an arm to Lettie. "She rides with me."

"Sir. . .please." Nathan's eyes widened in dismay. "We can't do that."

"Better ride right out in front of their noses." The elderly man slapped his hat back on his head. "Any of these wicked Burwells try to stop me, I'll shoot 'em dead."

When he patted a bulging pocket, Lettie understood that he meant his words.

Mr. Bryant hopped down. "Clever idea, sir. Capital!"

"What?" Nathan's eyes narrowed into slits. "It's ludicrous."

Bryant wiped his hands together. "No. Mr. Parkes can say he demands for Lettie to be there."

"Exactly." Mr. Parkes tugged Lettie's arm. They moved forward, the straw crunching under the thin soles of her house shoes.

Soon, Lettie found herself riding beside Charles City's notable plantation owner, clinging to the bench for dear life, as the man drove at a breakneck speed over the ruts of the country lanes. They drove past the edge of Burwell Plantation and the overseer scowled and yelled something at them.

Her grandpappy didn't slow at all, instead hooted in glee. "He'll be dead before morning."

Lettie's breath caught. She wasn't sure she'd heard correctly. Did he mean Mr. Burwell would be dead or the overseer? A chill shot through her clear to her toes.

"You don't mess with a Parkes unless you dare take on the consequences."

"Sir?"

He slowed the horses, deliberately glaring at the overseer. He transferred the reins to his other hand and tried to retrieve something from his navy silk waistcoat, a handsome garment. "Grab my flask, would ya, girl?"

Spying the silver cap, Lettie tugged it free.

Love's Escape

"Open it."

Spirits did awful things to white folks. But she did as commanded and handed it to him, still holding the cap.

"This here was from my great-grandfather. He fought in the American Revolution." Mr. Parkes drank from the container, gulping greedily. "He wanted freedom, yet he enslaved others."

Not knowing what to say, Lettie nodded then accepted the engraved flask back from him. She ran her finger over the figures of soldiers attired in breeches and hunting shirts, their muskets raised high.

"You keep that."

"I can't." Oh, no, she shouldn't have contradicted him. Would he hit her? She'd only twice talked back to the Burwell sons, and she'd paid for it with her flesh. She cringed at the memory and ducked, preparing for a blow that never came.

"It's yours. And much more." He directed the horse around a deep puddle in the road and slowed the wagon to a crawl.

Would Burwell send captors after them?

"What do you think Rush Parkes is telling Letitia?" The old man had surprised Nathan at every turn.

David hadn't appeared this twitchy since the first steeplechase they'd engaged in at school. "I hope he's saying something good."

"We cannot linger. We must get Letitia's mother buried and then be off."

"Humph! Try telling that old codger and see what he says." David shook his head.

They drove on past slaves toiling in the fields, as the sun beat down and evaporated the recent rain into a fog of steam. "How do they manage in this heat?"

57

"I don't know. It's unconscionable." Nathan loosened his collar.

"Yet our peers would continue this practice."

Nathan directed the horses to swerve around a deep rut. "Not only continue but pursue their 'property' up into the northern states and put teeth into the Fugitive Slave Act with hefty fines."

David grabbed the edge of his seat as the carriage slowed and dipped into the edge of the low-lying trench. "Do you believe the North will willingly cooperate with this new legislation?"

"It's not really new law but upping the ante for an old law on the books. And enforcing it."

"But will we get our ladies North only to have someone grab them and bring them back?" Hearing David give voice to the nagging worry aloud ignited a wave of fiery heat in his chest.

Nathan pulled at his collar, stopping when he felt a button begin to give way. He forced himself to calm. It wouldn't help anyone if he gave in to his emotions. "What kind of faith do we have if we can't trust God in every situation?" But his words sounded hypocritical. Hadn't he, himself, expressed these very concerns to David the entire way to Charles City? His face heated in embarrassment.

"We're told God can meet every need. But have you ever been tested before? Certainly on the high seas I have felt the Almighty's hand upon my ship in our worst hours—and I feel that direction now."

The wagon wheels churned on, the horses' hooves plodding through the thick Virginia soil.

Nathan had recently been nominated for deacon at Shockoe Baptist Church in Richmond. He'd grown up part of every activity offered in the church, home to some of Richmond's oldest and wealthiest families. What would the others say if they ever learned that Nathan had helped a slave escape and later

Love's Escape

married her? That *was* his plan, wasn't it? Was this truly the Lord's direction, too?

He exhaled a sigh. Yes, this had to be God's will.

"Beneida must be terrified in there."

Nathan flicked the reins, and the matched pair of bays picked up their pace. "I have an idea." How many nights had Nathan played out escape scenarios in his mind?

"Spit it out."

Mr. Parkes, who'd insisted Lettie call him "Grandpappy," had sent two house servants to pack a trunk for her and Beneida, then had sent them to change in a spacious room upstairs. The armoire held his daughter's and some of his granddaughter's clothing, which was faintly scented with cloves. The fabrics were fine, however the styles were quite out of fashion.

"We need to hurry, Beneida." Lettie longed to spend time gazing at her transformation in the long, silvered mirror in the blue flocked–wallpapered room. She fingered the gold necklace that her grandfather had pressed into her hand and that now hung from her neck, beads of deep blue lapis lazuli hanging in layers from the golden chain.

A knock on the door interrupted her reverie. "Time to go." Mr. Bryant's firm tone allowed no argument.

Beneida and Lettie grabbed their borrowed reticules.

Soon they'd descended the winding staircase, portraits of Lettie's ancestors looking on, free people who seemed to watch her escape. Were they nodding in approval? In the heavenly realms, did they watch like a great cloud of witnesses? She hoped so.

Nathan met her in the marble-floored entrance hall. "We have a plan. We can't waste time arguing."

"What?"

"Letitia, I'll need you to get into the coffin."

"No." Lettie shook her head so hard that the curls that Grandpappy Parkes' servant girl had coiled on her head began to loosen. She swiped at the deep coral skirt and white trimmed gown that Mr. Parkes had given her—one of his wife's that he'd kept. This elaborate ensemble hailed from the previous century but was in excellent condition. Only an older matron or an eccentric woman would be attired in such. "I'm not climbing into that casket, Nathan."

Beneida pushed a curl beneath her black bonnet. She patted the netted veil, held back by shiny ebony hat pins, and tied the ribbons at her chin. "It's not so bad."

"Then why were you white as a ghost when you got out?" Lettie fisted her hands on her hips, which were now almost twice as wide as normal, due to all the underpinnings she had and the extra material in the gown.

"At least you'll have more room up top." Beneida tugged at her black moiré sleeves. "I could hardly move at all in the bottom."

"I hate to ask this, but it's the best we can figure." Nathan's fond gaze stirred something in Lettie. Could she trust him? "And we must travel quickly."

"All right, then." Lettie lifted her skirts. Thankfully the fancy shoes she was given were only a little tight.

"We've put your bags in the hiding spot in the coffin." Mr. Bryant took Beneida's hand.

Nathan tucked Lettie's arm through his. "Let's practice descending the stairs together. We'll be doing this soon enough at the wharf."

Her cheeks heated as he drew her close to his side. His scent of leather and bayberry would be with her long after they parted. For no matter what he said, she'd not believe he would offer

Love's Escape

marriage to her. Not to an escaped slave. Still, they had to get to freedom. "Yes, let's do, for I'm afraid I may trip in these heels." And being treated like a lady felt altogether foreign.

Before long, they'd said their goodbyes to her grandpappy. How good of him to bury Mama in a proper manner, albeit in a simple pine casket. Now Lettie faced the wagon—and the coffin.

"Just jump on in the back."

How could she? Her dead mother had lain there.

"Do you know how many people have been conducted to freedom through our funeral parlor, my dear Letitia?"

She waved Nathan's comment away. "I don't care. I can't do it."

You can do this. The soft voice whispered to her soul.

Tears streaming down her cheeks, Lettie began to hum one of her favorite songs from church. And in no time at all, Nathan was assisting her into the box. His firm warm hands held hers as he tried to assist her.

"I need to lift you in." He released his hold and scooped her up, one strong arm beneath her legs and the other behind her shoulders like she was a bag of goose down.

She sucked in a breath and stared up at him as he lowered her into the fancy coffin. The padded satin lining felt cool, but Nathan's lips as he pressed a kiss to her forehead were hot.

"You'll be fine, Letitia. I'll be right here."

"Ready?" Mr. Bryant called out.

Nathan rolled a blanket up and lowered the coffin's top onto it, leaving space for air to circulate.

"Roll on!"

Within minutes, the carriage shuddered to a start, and Lettie slid slightly in the box. She cried out.

"Are you all right?"

"I'm fine. It's just slippery in here."

Nathan's fingers slid over the side and she reached through the gap created by the blanket roll and grasped them. While she yearned for the strength she felt there, she also knew her ideas of romance were foolish. But for now, she could pretend. She thought of the stories the Burwell sisters had enjoyed, many they'd read aloud while she dressed them or cleaned up after them. One was about a noble lady who was set adrift in a boat, and whose true love—a troubadour—found her and saved her from drowning in the shining lake. If she pretended that she was that lady, then maybe she'd not think about Mama lying on these same cushions.

They rode on, the sound of the wheels on the road faintly carrying into her hiding place.

Whose crazy idea was this? Nathan's back ached from sitting in the rear of the wagon on the ride to Richmond. Beneida, attired in a mourning gown belonging to one of the Parkes women, sat in the front with David, while Letitia lay in the top half of the coffin. This was his own notion, and a poor one.

"You there, Nathan?" Letitia's voice carried from the coffin. The bottom section had small holes drilled into it, but not the top—a defect Father would have to fix if they were to use this design again to carry a live person.

"I'm here."

Almost to Richmond, now, they'd not been accosted by anyone. Tomorrow, though, surely Burwell would seek the women out and demand to know where they were. Parkes swore he would claim that he had Letitia locked in his house and wasn't letting her out, and he'd deny knowing anything about Beneida. That might work for a few days until the sheriff was brought in to search.

Love's Escape

The scent of damp earth and brackish river water intensified as they neared the river. "We'll be there, shortly."

Soon, he'd be saying goodbye to his father, to Richmond and the South. He and David would take the two young women to freedom. First, though, they had to get safely home and then to the boat.

The carriage slowed. "Riders!" David called from the front.

Nathan jumped up, got his feet beneath him as the wagon swayed, and then pulled the blanket out that was holding the coffin open. "Just for precaution, Letitia."

"I'll lie real still."

"Sheriff Digges!" David's overly cheerful voice didn't hide the warning in his words. Nathan gently closed the coffin cover and sat on the blanket, on the wagon's bed.

They slowed to a stop.

"What are you doin' in the Pleasants' wagon?" Nathan strained to discern the owner of the stern voice. His heart hammered.

David said something back that was undecipherable.

"How you doin', Captain Bryant?" The other rider's voice resonated. Sheriff Digges of Richmond.

"Doing fine. Helping out Nate. He's in the back with this dear lady's departed kin." David's voice deepened in faux sympathy.

"My condolences, ma'am."

Thankfully, Nathan didn't hear Beneida reply, as they'd instructed her to remain quiet if they ran into any trouble.

"Her family asked if we'd allow her to ride with us to Richmond, so she could be there early. They'll be a few hours behind us."

"Checkin' in the back, Sheriff." In a moment, a mustached, ginger-haired man about Nathan's age peered in at him. He dismounted from his sorrel mare.

"Hello there. I'm Nathan Pleasant." He extended his hand, but the man narrowed his gaze.

"What ya got in that coffin?"

Nathan raised his eyebrows, feigning surprise. "A corpse."

"Don't suppose you'd mind if I looked?"

"Not at all. She doesn't stink." He winked. "Not yet."

The man blinked a few times. "I'm the new deputy. Barnes."

"Good to meet you, Deputy Barnes." A lie if ever there was one.

Barnes patted his mount's neck. "I heard one way to tell if the person in a casket is really dead is you can put a flame to their toe."

Chapter Six

Lettie gasped as she understood the muffled words. Would the deputy open the casket, remove her shoe, and place a flame on her foot? Would her gown light up in flames?

"That's right." Nathan's voice was even. "If the person is still alive, the burn will fill with fluid."

"Good way to check, ain't it?"

"It is. And my father does so as soon as we get the bodies to him, which you're preventing right now."

A long silence followed.

Dear God, please.

Finally, the sound of a second horse's hooves carried toward the back. Lettie shook from head to toe. Did she shake the wagon? She tried to breathe shallowly, but it was hard.

"What you yammerin' on about back here, Barnes?" The man's deep voice held authority.

"Just discussin' things." The deputy coughed.

"Time to get on our way as I'm sure these men ought."

"How's Mrs. Digges doing, Sheriff?"

"Fine, Nate. New baby is fine, too. Gracie won't be happy if we return after dark, though."

Nathan's laugh sounded genuine enough. "I'm just hoping my hindquarters aren't battered by the time we arrive in Shockoe."

"I'll take a long day on horseback over an afternoon in the back of a wagon any day."

"At least I'm not traveling that way!" Nathan's laughter was joined by the others. He must be pointing at the coffin.

Lettie wished she didn't have to travel this way, either.

"That's right, Nate. Now you stay outta that coffin, ya hear?"

"Sure thing, Sheriff. Have a safe journey."

"Safer than the ones we're going to get." Deputy Barnes' tone sent a chill down Lettie's spine.

"Mount up, Barnes."

The rustling of a saddle carried, and the horses whinnied.

She needed air. Her hands felt itchy, as though any moment they'd begin to tremble violently. She couldn't have anyone seeing her twitch. But had the deputy moved on? She must wait a moment before calling to Nathan.

"Letitia, I'll open that top just as soon as they're out of sight."

"Soon…please. It's hard to breathe." But every impact of hoofbeats, that carried the lawmen away, brought relief.

"How do you feel about being a widow, Letitia?"

"What?" She wasn't even married yet.

"I meant dressed in mourning—like Beneida is."

She'd not wanted to ask where they went next. Was afraid to hear the plan. Lettie ran her tongue over her lips to moisten them. The hearse bed creaked and the top of the coffin opened with a rush of light and fresh air. Nathan peered in, a concerned expression twisting his features. If the sight of her, lying in a coffin, didn't squelch any romantic notions he might have, then she didn't know what would.

He pressed a cool hand to her cheek. "Are you all right?"

"Yes," she whispered, sucking in the air, not minding the earthy smell of the dirt being kicked up behind the conveyance.

Nathan relished the feel of Letitia's soft skin. "I can't believe we did it."

"What?"

"Got both of you out of that plantation."

"I've been praying you'd come back for me." Letitia exhaled a sigh and a sob. "I'd just about given up. Was thinkin' about runnin' on my own."

"I'm glad you didn't. But I'm very sorry about your mother."

The familiar burning behind her eyes produced fresh tears. She sniffed.

"David never expected Beneida to return from England. He was sure she'd escape whilst in England."

"Too bad she didn't."

He shook his head. "I've never seen a man more heartsick than after her departure, that is until he'd heard she'd been sold and taken to Burwell Plantation."

"Would you have been heartsick if I'd left?"

His words stuck in his throat. *Devastated, not heartsick.*

When he didn't reply, Letitia closed her eyes, as though shutting him out.

"Moving on!" David called out.

"All right." He gazed down at the woman he loved.

"You best sit down, Nathan."

"Yes." He gently closed the lid onto the blanket.

"How you going to get us both out?"

"With two of you women, it will be a little more difficult, but David and I discussed a plan."

"We don't have to stay in this coffin, do we?"

"No." He exhaled sharply. "We considered that, but it would be too difficult. And risky."

"And I ain't doin' it. That's that."

He couldn't help laughing. "Well, let me tell you how things will go, once we get to my father's funeral home. He's affiliated with all of the larger churches in Richmond, and we conduct services and burials for those without any specific faith, as well."

For the next half hour, he explained to Letitia what would transpire. Then, when they arrived, his father and brother flew into action, helping the men transfer the casket inside, locking the room, and assisting Letitia out. Brief introductions were made.

Father's eyes widened as he took in Letitia's appearance. "With her light coloring, she could easily walk around Richmond on your arm and no one would know she was a slave."

"That's true, but Letitia has visited the town with Nanny Burwell. She'll need a disguise."

"We're not risking anyone recognizing either of our precious ladies." David lifted a deep purple gown from the trunk.

"Have you got another heavy veil in there, Father?"

"For you, Son, I'd steal one from our patrons if necessary."

They embraced.

"I'll miss you, Father."

"Don't come back."

The parrot fluttered its wings and squawked, "Don't come back." Seemed he and his father both agreed on that.

Everything happened in such a rush that Lettie felt dizzy as the two couples were soon outside again, this time heading toward the wharf and a ship that would carry them to freedom. She tugged at the bottom of the scratchy black veil that smelled of someone's face powder. She fought the urge but then sneezed through the face covering, sending a tiny puff of white powder forward.

Nathan squeezed her hand.

Love's Escape

"Mrs. Scholtus," Nathan said her fake name so convincingly, Lettie almost believed she was the widow Mary Scholtus. "We'll get you down to the boat, where you'll soon be home to your family."

"I do miss Philadelphia." A place she'd never been and could scarcely believe she would soon see.

Nathan brushed a piece of lint from his navy-and-gray herringbone wool suit. "Pity it's not for a leisurely visit."

Ahead of them, Beneida slowed. "Will your father be able to get our belongings to the ship?"

"He's already sent the carter with them, but they'll be traveling on the main road while we're taking these two backstreets for the moment."

Soon they turned up a side street toward their destination. The brackish water of the river filled the air, dampening her clothes, but not Lettie's rising hopes. Her heartbeat hammered out time with their quick footsteps as they stepped up onto the wooden walkway.

"We won't be on this route for long. There's a step down ahead." Nathan pointed to where the walkway ended and a bricked path extended to the wharf.

Pipe and cigar smoke wafted up from a side green, where a group of a dozen men, all similarly attired in waistcoat, jacket, slim trousers, and buffed shoes, gathered. Southern men who would seek to keep her enslaved. Yes, many spoke out against slavery, but the plantation owners' voices prevailed. They needed the slaves to hold onto their livelihoods and prosperity.

Just ahead of them, Captain Bryant and Beneida strode more quickly, the thick dark mesh of the dark-haired woman's veil covering her face and neck and the extra padding in her gown making her appear more like a matron than the young woman she was.

"It's all been so tedious. So tiresome." Beneida's affectatious voice sounded a cross between a Southern lady and a rich Northerner. "I'll feel so much better when we've put this ordeal behind us."

Lettie clung to Nathan's arm, periodically glancing around them. Ahead, ships six deep stood over two-stories high on the water. She'd never been on a ship before. Would they sink in a storm? She bit back the urge to laugh. For she could smell freedom: like horses, straw, the wool of another's fine garment, and the spicy scent of Nathan Pleasant.

She lifted her head higher. She was a lady. A grieving lady. Mrs. Scholtus. It didn't take much for the tears to stream as she remembered what her mother had endured. She reached into her reticule for a handkerchief. A real linen handkerchief. Embroidered with someone else's initials, but it didn't matter.

As they neared the dock, a stream of dark-skinned slaves were unloaded, some barely dressed and then only in rags. Lettie gasped.

Nathan patted her hand. "Don't be alarmed, dear. I'm sure there's no problem here."

Beneida, too, held fast to her escort's arm.

"There's the passenger's queue." Nathan pointed ahead to where a line of men, women, and children meandered forward toward a ship.

All manner of crew ran up and down the boarding planks and hauled luggage back on.

Mr. Bryant smiled over his shoulder. "I was told they intend to depart promptly."

Good. The sooner they left, hopefully the quicker this churning in her gut would stop.

"You, there!" A man's low voice called out behind them.

Love's Escape

Nathan continued walking. "Keep going," he hissed. "Just ignore him."

Captain Bryant stepped aside, with Beneida. "Get onto the ship, you two. Remember our plan."

"Bryant!" The man behind them called more urgently.

Nathan grasped her hand and pulled Lettie onward, toward the gangplank. Soon the line slowed as tickets were collected.

"Ticket?" The swarthy man, a head shorter than Nathan, frowned at Lettie, who was dabbing at her cheeks beneath the borrowed veil.

"Here you are." Nathan passed the passes to the man.

As they were waved on, Lettie tugged at Nathan's arm. "We can't leave Beneida and Mr. Bryant."

Nathan grinned at her. "They can't leave without the captain aboard." But sweat trickled down his brow.

Lettie turned to see a red-faced man shaking a finger at David Bryant, while Beneida took a step backward.

Chapter Seven

Atlantic Ocean
Off the Eastern seaboard of America

Lettie cradled Beneida's head in her lap and pushed damp curls away from her flushed forehead. "You'll be all right soon enough." As soon as this ship came ashore. But then there'd be another host of problems.

"You feeling better, yourself?" Her friend's whisper was raw as a freshly pulled potato from the ground.

"Yes, thanks to you." Lettie grabbed the nearby cup of ginger tea. "Sit up a little bit and drink."

The ship's gentle rocking motion sloshed a bit of liquid onto the pastel quilt that covered the women. But the herbal tea's action was nothing compared to the terrifying waves they'd tossed through the previous night. Only Captain Bryant resisted the ocean sickness that had overcome the rest of them. How was Nathan faring today? They'd sent a man in to sit with him but had heard no word this morning.

Beneida took a few sips but then pressed the cup back into Lettie's hand. "Thank you."

Lettie set the medicinal drink back on the small mahogany table next to the bed. Then she helped her friend lie back down. She pulled the coverlet up over Beneida's quivering shoulders.

"I think I can sleep now, Lettie."

Love's Escape

Would her friend's dreams be filled with Captain Bryant as Lettie's were with Nathan? All of their promises seemed to be coming true. She couldn't help dreaming that one day she might have a husband as kind as Nathan Pleasant. What would it be like to be Mrs. Pleasant? A tear slipped down her face.

He'd never said he loved her—only that he cared for her deeply. And the brave man had never promised her more than assisting her to escape, unlike the promises David Bryant had made to Beneida.

The dark-haired man had dropped down on bended knee the previous evening and presented Beneida with a beautiful garnet ring. The pursuer who'd flagged them down at the wharf was the jeweler who had taken the captain's order months earlier, before Beneida had departed for England. The shop owner had certainly given them all a good scare, chasing after the captain like that to make sure he took possession of the ring, for which David had already paid.

Lettie waited, and when Beneida's breath became gentler and even with sleep, she rose and quietly washed up, using one of the fresh towels that the captain had sent in that morning. How nice to have a clean fresh cloth and soap that smelled of lemons. Lettie lifted the soap bar to her nose and sniffed. She smiled. As the ship rose on a swell, she braced her feet, glad she'd remembered to fill the water basin only shallowly for just this reason.

She slowly opened the lid of the black leather–wrapped trunk that her grandfather had sent with them, which squeaked a slow moan. When Beneida stirred in the bed, Lettie held still, praying the woman would not awaken.

After a moment of silence, save for the groaning of the ship, Lettie pulled a chemise; an overblouse in an interwoven lavender, black, and deep purple linen with ribbon trim; and a matching plum-colored skirt from the trunk. Mr. Parkes's daughters had owned beautiful clothing. Even with these colors of late mourning, the ensemble was stylish. With a little stitching, Beneida and she could alter the clothing to fit them. If they stopped at a millinery shop, they could even choose updated ribbons and laces to bedeck their gowns. Lettie ran her hands over the finely woven chemise and pulled it over her head, recalling a visit to Richmond during which Mrs. Burwell had allowed her to select a satin ribbon for herself. She'd chosen a narrow burgundy strand, which she had given to her mother. Mama had cried when Lettie pressed it into her chafed hands.

Tears streamed down Lettie's face as she dressed herself. Here she was wearing ladies' clothing. Her mother lay dead. These garments had been worn by her blood relations. Women who solely by birth were free, while Mama was enslaved and then sold off to the neighbors.

Mama would have said, "Ain't no use worryin' about what has gone by. Trust the good Lord. One day we'll all be free in glory." Lettie wiped away the tears and sniffed before glancing in the mirror.

Her cheeks, as pale as any white woman's, were streaked with red from crying. Her hair needed a good brushing. She reached for the brand-new, boar-bristle brush that sat atop the dressing table. There was a matching one for Beneida. Each had her own. Lettie ran her fingers over the rosewood handle—as fine as Mrs. Burwell's brush.

Hope, like a kindling, a tiny spark lighting the hearth, rose up within her. Something she'd never felt before bubbled in her. What was it?

Joy. Joy despite the hardships. Joy rising above the fear.

Lettie blinked back more tears and raised a hand to her lips to stifle a laugh. Beneida had been the only enslaved young woman Lettie knew who seemed happy. Who spoke of joy. At least she had, the few times they'd met in Richmond.

She set the hairbrush back down and retrieved a handkerchief, blowing her nose as quietly as she could. The new emotion made her suck in a breath. From her first memories, all she had known was bondage, of being made to sit still and watch as her mother worked. To stay out of the way. To see her mother mistreated by people who said they owned her. And look what Beneida's owners had done.

Only I own you. If you choose. There'd been no audible voice. Just a whispering inside her. In her soul.

She sighed and lifted the hairbrush to her head, removing tangles as quickly as she could. She gathered and pinned her tresses into what she hoped would pass for a lady's hairstyle. She'd often done the elder Mrs. Burwell's silver tresses in such a fashion. She didn't mind being considered dowdy as long as she wasn't caught as an escaped slave.

Soon she was ready to check on Nathan. First, she leaned over Beneida, then extinguished the oil lamp before leaving the room and locking the door. Outside, the skies were heavily overcast with thick gray clouds piled up on top of one another like pillows awaiting a good beating. She held the railing affixed to the ship's side, as Captain Bryant had instructed her to do, even though the waters were calm.

A worker walked by, balancing a tray in one hand. He nodded and bowed his head in subservience, avoiding her inquisitive glance. How strange to have a servant treat her like a superior. She wasn't, of course.

How odd to be treated as a free woman.

Could it last?

Between the bell clanging, a horn tooting from the Philadelphia harbor, and the noise of shipmen clattering up and down the stairs, Nathan's ears rang.

Porters rushed past Nathan on the ship's passageway; their carts piled high with luggage. "Make way! Make way!"

This was real—they had sailed upriver into Philadelphia's fine harbor, its long, wide wharf a welcoming beehive of activity on the land below.

David strode toward him, still attired in his captain's clothing. He clapped his hands together. "I'm ready for some good Philadelphia cooking." Only the tic near his left eye gave away his anxiety.

"Let's gather our good ladies, then."

The two of them carefully zigzagged between the passengers and crew members, most making way when they eyed David's uniform. The captain grinned and tipped his hat at all the women as they passed.

Finding the appropriate cabin, Nathan knocked on the escaped slaves' door. In a moment, it opened, and the two, their faces obscured by the heavy black veils, emerged from the cabin. He tucked Lettie's gloved hand into the crook of his arm. "Ready?"

"You have no idea how ready I am."

He chuckled. "I believe I have a notion."

Beneida eyed Nathan. "You're looking mighty spry for having been so ill, Mr. Pleasant."

"That's because you're viewing my friend through a veil, my dear." David patted his sweetheart's arm. "He's still a dull shade of gray-green."

"Much like the skies, then." Letitia pointed overhead to where the dark clouds gleamed the sickly color.

Love's Escape

Soon they descended from the ship. The sun forced its way out from beneath the banked rain clouds, the fragile rays illuminating the small group.

"A good omen, I pray." Nathan resisted the urge to pick Letitia up and swirl her around.

David bent and embraced Beneida. "We're here, my beloved."

Looking up through the dark veil, Letitia grinned.

Nathan gently lifted the veil and pressed a kiss to her smooth forehead, enjoying her soft gasp of surprise. He quickly lowered the dark mesh, again. "The city of brotherly love."

Letitia cocked her head at him.

"That's the meaning of the city's name," he explained.

"Oh."

David leaned in. "How does it feel to be in one of the largest cities in our great nation? Over a hundred thousand people live here, I've heard."

Fantastic? Frightening? Freeing? How did Letitia feel?

"Good place to disappear." Letitia's soft voice barely carried over the loud noises of the carters as they rolled baggage from the docks, the passengers conversing loudly with one another, and street vendors hawking wares.

The scent of sausages cooking over charcoal wafted toward them.

David jerked a thumb toward them. "Shall we?"

No doubt the women wished to flee the wharf as quickly as possible. But he and David had cautioned the two that they must act naturally.

Still, his friend continued to scan faces at the dock. "I saw no one I recognized on board nor on the roster of travelers."

"I'm not yet well enough to eat. I'll leave my veil on." Beneida turned from David to watch the passengers who streamed past.

Letitia jostled Nathan's arm. "Why don't you men have your sausages, and then let's go on to the inn?"

Nathan's stomach rumbled, and despite his seasickness, his empty gullet begged to be filled. "We'll have something sent upstairs for you ladies when we arrive at our lodgings."

They all stepped closer to where a man, attired in heavy wool garments, poked at the sausages sizzling on a grate over a bed of coals. David held up two fingers and pointed to the sausages.

When the vendor muttered something back in what sounded like German, Nathan looked to his friend. David, however, was already fishing money out of his embossed leather wallet and handing it to the vendor.

"I've never seen sausages served like this." Letitia pointed to the thick split rolls upon which the man placed the links.

Nathan grinned at her. "Do you want to try it?"

"Maybe a bite?"

"Here, take your gloves off. Then you can manage if you push that veil up." He assisted her in unbuttoning the wrists and tugging each tight finger free from the gloves. Even with all the bustle of people coming and going on the wharf, the act felt intimate.

But this was as a husband should do for his wife, was it not?

"Thank you." Letitia's throaty whisper caused his cheeks to heat.

"You're welcome, my love."

Her eyes widened in surprise. It was the first time he'd used that word with her. Was it possible that she might welcome a life spent with him? Did she care for him more than just as a friend who'd help her escape to freedom? He raised her hand to his lips and pressed a kiss to her hand, inhaling the sweet scent of lemons.

"Why, Nathan. . ." Letitia's accent grew more affected.

So, she was just playing the part. Disappointment riffled through him.

A chill breeze nearly lifted his hat, and he grabbed it and pushed it back down, his senses on alert. Father had given permission for them to seek out abolitionist William Still, if they encountered any difficulties here. He'd also warned Nathan that to do so could also endanger their mission and to contact him only if in dire circumstances.

From a nearby bank of low wooden structures, a man attired in a loose-sleeved shirt, a snug brown vest, and matching pants exited and jogged in their direction. Nathan's heartbeat ratcheted up.

"It's just one of our shoremen," David muttered. "Be calm."

The tousle-haired man slowed as he neared. Breathing heavily, he shoved a telegram at David. "Captain, this just arrived for you."

His friend scanned the message. "It's from your father, Nate."

"What does it say?"

"He says your two stray cats want sardines, but he fed them Irish stew and he'll keep doing so."

Beneida snorted. "What kind of crazy talk is that?"

"It's a coded message." David drew in a deep breath.

Nathan rubbed his temple. "It's a warning."

Chapter Eight

Nathan's chest squeezed. "It means two people were looking for you ladies and that Father was giving them malarkey, a bit of the Blarney stone, to deter them."

The German vendor glanced up, thick brows drawn together. Did he understand English? Nathan would have to be more careful what he said in public.

"Did he say anything else?" Letitia wrung her hands.

David lifted the telegram. "He hopes your holiday to *Boston* gives you a little rest."

Boston meant they couldn't stay on the Eastern seaboard but to deter to Buffalo. And 'a little rest' meant they might have pursuers a few days behind them.

"Boston?" Beneida clutched her reticule tighter.

He and David would have to discuss their change of plans in private. They would have to be very careful. They'd discussed David obtaining a sailing position to France, but he wasn't sure he could find a ship quickly enough. How would Nathan support himself, though? He had nothing beyond the savings they'd use to get them to Buffalo and for provision for several months afterward. He needed to be able to take care of Letitia—if she'd allow him. She may wish to taste fully of freedom, though, before being tied down, and he understood that. For now, they needed to get to safety and then reevaluate.

Love's Escape

"Let's all have a sit-down." David pointed to two benches in a small grassy area ten paces beyond the vendor's cart.

After they'd finished eating, the foursome walked out to the main thoroughfare.

Cholera Kills 5,000 in New York! So proclaimed the front of the newspaper held aloft in a young lad's hand.

Nathan handed the coin to the child, filthy rags wrapped around his hands for warmth. Nathan removed his leather gloves and handed them to the boy. "Promise me you won't sell these but keep them for yourself."

Pale blue eyes widened in surprise, or perhaps that was distrust.

David sighed loudly. "Young Sean. If I return to port and find you've pawned them, I'll box your ears myself."

"You know this boy?" Nathan swiveled to face his friend.

"He's the tavern girl's son and I always save an extra bit of lunch for him when I'm in port." David pulled his half-eaten sandwich from his coat pocket and handed that and a coin to the thin boy. *So, David hadn't finished his lunch.*

Sean tucked the gloves in his pocket and shoved the half-sandwich in his mouth.

Beneida stepped forward. "Not too quickly, child, you'll choke on that."

Nathan straightened, surprised by the confidence in the woman's voice. Likely due to how the Dolleys had treated her. Perchance this young woman could help Letitia find her way, too.

David hailed a passing coach and the men assisted the ladies inside.

"The *Das Geheime Inn*," David told the driver.

Once inside the vehicle, Nathan tipped his chin up toward his friend. "The driver didn't have any reaction to where we're going. So that's good. Right?"

David shrugged. "I've stayed there many times, and even I didn't know this was a conductor's safe place until your father told me."

Letitia peered out the windows as they rolled down the cobblestone streets. Her eyes grew wider as they passed freedmen and women walking to businesses along the thoroughfare. Most were attired in warm modest clothing, definitely not slave garb, with fashionable hats.

Beneida smiled. "It was like this in England. There were no slaves unless someone had brought them, as the Dolleys had me. And I spied many free people of color in the business districts."

The carriage made a tight turn down a narrow street.

"Your destination," the driver called out as he pulled alongside the inn.

David disembarked from the carriage and assisted Beneida. Then Nathan jumped down and helped Letitia, relishing the feel of her hand in his. When he smiled at her, she blushed. Did she feel the same affection, and attraction, toward him as he did toward her?

The skies had darkened again. "Let's get inside before it pours." Raindrops began to plop onto the brick sidewalk that led to the two-story, square inn sided in white clapboard. Heavy dark green shutters, held open by S-shaped brass holders affixed to the house's exterior, reminded him that this port, this city, like Virginia, also experienced hurricanes.

At least they didn't have to go back out onto the ocean again. *Thank God for that.* Apparently Father's sea legs had not been passed on to Nathan.

"Hurry!" Beneida encouraged.

They stepped into the building just as the clouds opened and poured their contents down. Nathan quickly secured the front

Love's Escape

door, then turned to inhale the heavy fragrance of apples and cinnamon inside the cozy establishment.

To the left, tables and chairs filled a small room that could hold perhaps twenty people but currently lay empty.

David swiveled to face him. "They serve only breakfast and dinner here, but I'm sure Mrs. Frohlich will have the kitchen send something up."

"I can wait." Beneida placed a hand on her padded stomach. She certainly looked the part of a matronly woman.

"Me, too." Letitia tugged at her hatstrings. "I have got to get this contraption off my head."

The wide-brimmed black bonnet, to which the veil was affixed, did look heavy and uncomfortable.

Footsteps sounded on the nearby staircase. A blue shirt strained across the chest of a blond workman. He looked half a head taller than both Nathan and David. "Travelers?"

"Yes," all four exhaled the word simultaneously.

The worker eyed David. "I'm Johan Frolich. Do you remember me?"

"You're the owner's son, yes?"

"*Ja.*" Light blue-gray eyes swept over the other three. "They also enjoy the daffodils, ja?"

The four of them nodded as Nathan raised a fist overhead, exulting in obtaining the first step of Letitia's freedom. "Ja!"

Lettie shivered as she washed. Morning light filtered through the broadcloth curtains that ran from ceiling to floor. Behind the ugly brown cloth, reminiscent of slaves' clothing, harbor winds rattled the two tall windows. Lettie bent over the basin and dipped her cloth into the chill water she'd poured from the old-fashioned creamware pitcher.

"Where will we go today?" Beneida threw back the down-stuffed bedcovers and stretched, her mussed black curls trailing down her slim back. She tugged at the shoulders of her linen gown.

Lettie eyed the dresses hanging in the open mahogany wardrobe. Never in her life had she owned so many clothes. But when she wore them, she would have to settle into the garments so she didn't appear uncomfortable.

A gentle tap at the door startled her and Lettie sloshed water onto the front of her chemise. She dropped her rag into the water and leaned heavily against the washstand. Had someone discovered them? "Who be—"

"You know," the low, deep voice was unrecognizable, and her heart lurched in her chest.

"Who?" she managed.

"It's me, David," the captain whispered through the door. "We'll meet you in the dining hall in twenty minutes."

Beneida ran to the door. "Yes, dearest." Her singsong voice made Lettie laugh.

"We'll eat without you if you're late, so no dawdling." *My, he sounded stern.*

Beneida just laughed.

The captain's footsteps echoed down the hall.

"He acts like he's your husband already." Or how Lettie imagined husbands might act. From what she'd seen of the plantation owners and their wives she'd found it shocking that Phebe Burwell would ever want to be wed. Then again, she'd likely wanted to flee from her father.

"I doubted him for too long, Lettie. Don't you make the same mistake." The beautiful woman shook a finger at her. "I can tell Nathan cares for you deeply. If I'd only believed that of

Love's Escape

David, we might have escaped long ago and I'd not be placing you in peril."

Lettie dipped her chin, feeling chastened. Who was Beneida to tell her what she should do? Lettie would be free to make her own choices.

"I'm sorry. I spoke out of turn." Beneida huffed a sigh. "I just feel so badly that now instead of just you and Nathan traveling it's the four of us."

"Maybe that's better, though. I mean, wouldn't people be less likely to question two couples than one?"

Beneida's dark eyebrows drew together. "Maybe so."

"Come on. Let's get dressed."

"And wear our matching velvet hats with feather plumes." Beneida grinned as she donned her outfit.

Soon, the two women descended the stairs to the dining room.

Both men rose from the table overlooking the street. Outside, early morning street sweepers worked, and carters hauled luggage, vegetables, and all manner of caged animals up the busy street. As a goose determinedly flapped its wings inside a crate, Lettie shivered. Nathan followed her gaze, his eyes half closed, as though he realized the reason for her distress.

He pulled her chair back and assisted her into it.

Leaning close, his warm breath caressed her ear. "You are not a caged goose, Lettie."

She stiffened.

"We depart earlier on the train than planned," he whispered.

"For Boston?"

"Buffalo."

But what of the cholera epidemic? Had they not considered that? Would they travel to freedom only to die of that dread disease?

85

Across the table, David assisted his "wife" into her spot and gave her a husbandly peck on the cheek. "How are you feeling this morning, my darling?"

Heat flushed Lettie's cheeks. Nathan took his seat next to her. He pressed an unusually chill hand over hers. "We believe we've attracted attention."

Lettie drew in a full breath; glad she'd not taken time to don one of the infernal corsets that Beneida insisted upon her wearing.

Captain Bryant leaned in. "We saw two men lingering outside the hotel this morning."

"I thought I recognized one." Nathan released her hand. "I can't place him, though.

"I'm hoping he's a doppelgänger." The captain pressed his lips together.

"A what?" Lettie scowled but then forced her features to relax. Ladies didn't scowl. At least not in public they didn't. So many new rules she'd needed to learn.

Nathan tapped his fingers on the table. "It means a person who looks like someone else."

"Like a cousin?" She'd noticed that many of the Burwell cousins could pass as brothers or sisters.

"Like that, but it usually means someone who looks like a double of you but is of no relation."

Who were her relatives? The Burwells' faces danced through Lettie's mind. What common features did they all share? But they were not related for purposes of the world. She was a slave. And they were her owners. Moisture pricked her eyes, and she swiped it away with the back of her hand.

"Here." Nathan tugged a creamy handkerchief from his jacket pocket and passed it to her, his touch definitely cool. He must be frightened, too. But a man wasn't allowed to show it.

Love's Escape

Maybe though, it was only the chill morning air causing his cold hands.

"The proprietor wasn't here when the two gentlemen were lingering, so we couldn't ask him who they might be." David ran his hand over his jawline. "But we'll take the train as soon as possible."

"We have to learn how soon that would be." Nathan brushed at his vest.

"Couldn't we at least do a quick tour of the Philadelphia sights?" Beneida leaned in toward Mr. Bryant. "Isn't this city one of the seats of freedom for this country?"

Not for slaves.

"Let us out at Independence Hall." Nathan instructed the cabdriver before they got in. Soon, they'd arrived at the imposing building. A thrill shot through him at the thought of bringing independence to these two women. With a delay until they could depart on a train, they'd planned some quick, but hopefully meaningful excursions.

"The bell is in the Assembly Room downstairs. Just follow us." David took Beneida's arm and entered the brick building.

"Mr. Burwell used to say they ought to crack the bell all the way through now that people are using it as a symbol of freedom from slavery." Letitia's voice held barely repressed anger.

What must it be like to have a father who was your owner and kept you enslaved?

Nathan cleared his throat. "The abolitionists have, indeed, grasped onto the bell as a representation of their cause."

"Which makes it all the more fitting that we view this symbol before departing." Beneida's smile grew tight.

"I'm glad they moved it to where more people can now view it," David called over his shoulder.

They moved toward a queue of visitors. Before too long, the four stood before the icon. Displayed on an ornate sculpted eagle stand, the cracked Liberty Bell rang something true, something real, within Nathan's heart.

"Do you feel it?" Letitia whispered.

"I do." He wrapped an arm around her.

Beneida and Letitia stood stiffly, staring at the large bell. The woman he loved deserved freedom. All enslaved people deserved to be free. How could this country call itself one representing independence when they continued to keep others of a different color in bondage?

"Not particularly so beautiful to look upon, but altogether lovely in what it represents." David placed his free hand over his heart.

"It's lovely, Captain Bryant." Letitia's eyes glistened.

"Please, call me David." He smiled. "I am, after all, betrothed to your best friend."

"Thank you. . . David." The hitch in her voice caused something in Nathan to also clench.

Behind them, the voices of those awaiting their turn rose slightly, likely signaling their impatience.

"As much as I hate to be rushed," Beneida turned and cast a sharp gaze at those standing behind them, "I believe we must move on."

"Agreed. And although I hate to do so, I must leave you all now to get our tickets." Nathan took Letitia's arm and led her away from the symbol of precious liberty, with David and Beneida following.

"I'll keep my eyes open for those men." David perused the hall slowly. "And if I see them, we'll take refuge at the Quakers' Hall."

Love's Escape

"I'll stop to look for you at the Merchants' Exchange first, though." Nathan nodded to David, who had suggested the beautiful building would be a good stop and he could check on his stocks while he was there.

He released Letitia's arm, immediately feeling the absence of her warmth, beside him. As he looked down into those beautiful green eyes, was that love that he saw reflecting back?

He took her hand and pressed a kiss to it. Nathan hurried off through the morning crowds to the train station. Cigar smoke, body odors, and manure in the street comingled with sea air and vendor's food booths. Soon he'd reached his destination and he entered the building.

The bespectacled ticket booth clerk tapped his black visor. "This one departs at 1:00 sharp, young man. Today only." His light eyes fixed on Nathan's. "You can make changes up the line."

"Yes, sir." He paid. But they had much farther to go from that stop.

Nathan first checked the Merchants' Exchange. He dodged passengers and traffic as he crossed one busy street after another.

A dray pulled out from the curb just as Nathan was stepping past and his heart lurched in his chest. He cast an angry glance at the driver, who was raining down curses on him.

Wouldn't that be something? Mowed over by draft horses before they could ever get the women to safety.

Nathan tugged at his cravat that had come loose from its butterfly tie and tapped his top hat as he reentered the building. Men dressed in business attire crowded the place.

Attired in her dusky lavender dress, Letitia stood by the far wall gazing at a painting of a patrician Philadelphian. She turned and met his gaze. His breath stuck in his throat. Her auburn curls trailed down her creamy skin, visible above the bodice of her waist-nipping jacket. *Dear Lord, You've made her so beautiful, so kind, so persistent, and filled with a passion for knowing You better. How could You allow her to be enslaved?*

All were God's children. What would it take? Talking hadn't worked. With this new act, or rather the enforcement of an old law, would words turn to something worse? Could reason not prevail?

David and Beneida rose from where they occupied a low divan. "Isn't it grand, Nate?"

"An imposing building to be sure."

From the corner of his eye, Nathan sensed movement. He swiveled, expecting to spy the two men whose path crossing theirs earlier. His hands fisted.

Instead, a well-dressed older man locked eyes with Nathan. He smiled and cocked his head before lifting his bowler hat in acknowledgement. He stepped forward, his focus on the handkerchief peeking from Nathan's pocket.

A handkerchief embroidered with a yellow daffodil.

The stranger wore a similar one.

Who was Nathan chatting with? Lettie lifted the watch pinned on her bodice. It felt so strange to have the heavy timepiece there. They hadn't much time to spare, did they? Should she play the adoring wife and join Nathan? Before she could decide, David and Beneida joined her.

David smiled down at her. "Have no worries. That man poses us no harm."

"Who is he?"

"Do you see the daffodil embroidered on his handkerchief?"

Lettie peered around David's broad shoulders. "I can't tell from here."

"Well, he has one. As does Nathan, if you've ever looked closely on this trip."

"I hadn't noticed."

Beneida leaned into the captain. "Is he a fellow conductor?"

"Yes." A muscle jumped in the man's cheek.

David took their elbows and steered them toward the exit.

Lettie stopped walking, and he released her. "You're leavin' my Nathan here?" Her cheeks heated. She'd just called Nathan Pleasant *hers*. He was no more hers, than she was his.

"Only for a moment."

She puffed out an exasperated breath as they exited the building and went out near the street. Wagon wheels rattled over cobblestones. Vendors called out their wares. Men and women ambled, arm in arm, some veering from beggars with hands outstretched.

A flaxen-haired girl ducked in front of Lettie, front teeth missing in her dirt-streaked face revealing her to be about six years old. "Got a half-penny, lady?"

David scowled as Lettie struggled with her pouch and fished out a coin. As quickly as the half-penny had dropped into the tiny palm, the child was gone.

"Mind yourself, Miss Letitia, for some of these urchins will rob you just like that!" He snapped his fingers.

"I've only seen such children at the wharves." Beneida's black eyebrows rose high. "Never in Richmond proper."

The few times Lettie had been to the Virginia capital, she'd been more concerned about how to escape than she had been about noticing any of the unfortunate children. Old Mrs. Burwell remarked that at least the slaves were fed and housed and clothed, unlike the cast-off children who'd likely die in a gutter before they'd reached ten years of age. Lettie's hands trembled, recalling her thoughts that she'd rather be free like those urchins and live a short life than to die a slave. *Was such a thought wicked, Lord? Do You have a reason for my life?*

"I've asked the hotel porter to transport our luggage to the railroad. But we paid for an extra night." David's eyes lowered to half-closed.

"What of the porter? Did you pay for his silence?" Beneida gazed up at David.

They stopped walking and stepped aside so an elderly couple could pass, the silver-haired gentleman giving David a sharp look.

"What have we to keep silent, wife?" David issued a short chuckle.

"True. We are simply a couple traveling with our friends on holiday."

"And if we act as if we've changed our minds, that is fine."

"But the hotel fee?" Lettie frowned.

"Ah." David stroked his chin. "Better a happy and *quiet* innkeeper who has received his full pay for our board than one vexed at losing the income from two days' rent."

"Even if Mr. Frohlich is a cooperator, and an abolitionist, he must earn a living." Beneida bobbed her head as if agreeing with herself.

Lettie shook her head at what seemed such a waste of good money. "I'm grateful, David, that you know about such things." As much sorrow, as much toil, as much denial as she'd experienced, Lettie was as wise in the way of the world as a baby lamb was.

When they continued on and reached the intersection, David led them away from the railroad station. "We're to take lunch at the Philadelphia Tavern."

Lettie stiffened. She wanted to protest but she didn't want to anger the captain. "I don't know if I'll be able to fit in these fine new clothes if the food at the tavern is as good as you say."

Love's Escape

"Do we have time for this?" Beneida glanced to the left and right.

Carefully, Lettie took in the approaching walkers. Two women who looked to be sisters, with identical light-brown hair curling around matching round, thin-lipped faces briskly strolled past. A Quaker minister, wearing an odd-looking hat, passed them and then turned down a walkway to the meeting hall.

How strange to be walking in public and sharing a walkway with people. A woman dressed in brown homespun fabric approached them, holding tightly to the hands of two young dark-haired boys. Both children were attired in coal-black knickers and white cotton shirts. They struggled to pull free. One threw himself down in front of them and they stopped.

"Sorry," the plain woman muttered to them as she sank to retrieve the child.

"Do you need help?" Lettie bent over.

The woman didn't respond to Lettie's question, instead focused on the flailing child. She released the hand of the boy.

The child ran to Lettie, clutched her knees, and gazed up. "Pretty. Like Mama."

The boy had dark wavy locks and striking blue eyes in his rosy face. Could she have a child so handsome? Lettie lifted him up onto one hip, as she'd done with the Burwell children, and jostled him there.

He placed his hands on her cheeks and pressed them, intently examining her face. "Mama's gone."

Tears clouded her vision.

Her mother was gone, as well. Brutally murdered in front of a crowd of witnesses. Hot tears poured down her cheeks.

"Miss Letitia," David hissed, his face flushed. "Don't make a spectacle of yourself."

The stranger gathered the other child up. "I'm sorry. They're due for a nap, and I kept them out too long."

"Can we help get them home?" Lettie avoided David's gaze but heard his loud sigh.

The woman, who must be the boys' caregiver, glanced at them but shook her head. "My employer wouldn't be happy." She extended her free hand and the child shuffled off toward her.

"Goodbye pretty lady," the little boy called out as the nanny walked off.

The captain turned on Lettie. "What were you thinking?"

She shrugged.

"It's thoughtlessness like that that will derail this journey."

Beneida gave a curt laugh.

"What's so funny?"

"Letitia was being thoughtful, yet you called her helping that governess a thoughtless act."

He curled his lips together. "That isn't what I meant, and you know it."

Footfall on the cobblestones behind them carried toward them. The trio turned.

Nathan ran to catch up. "Did you see them?"

"Who?" David tilted his head and looked back.

"The two men from this morning."

"No." Lettie lowered her head and sent up a quick prayer.

David shook his head. "Didn't see them."

"They are definitely following in our footsteps."

"Let's take the back alley to the tavern." The captain took Beneida's hand and quickly turned the corner.

Nathan likewise took Lettie's and somehow she felt safe again, with this man at her side. Safer, anyway, than she would feel without his presence.

Love's Escape

Soon they'd entered the well-appointed tavern. Letitia took in the beautiful paintings, the gilded frames, the expensive mahogany furniture. Tall windows, draped in heavy velvet curtains, allowed ample light to pool on the burgundy patterned wool rugs. *I don't belong here. I'm not fooling anyone.* She swallowed hard.

Captain Bryant pressed his broad hands on her and Beneida's backs. "Go out the tavern's back door."

"Hurry!" Nathan encouraged. "Go on to the railroad by yourselves while we distract them."

Could they? Or would their pursuers overtake them in the alley?

Lettie's heart pounded as she and Beneida strode past the tables, with diners giving them sideways glances. She had to trust Nathan.

Behind them, the captain greeted someone.

Beneida groaned.

"What is it?"

"That's a cockney accent."

Some sort of Englishmen were chasing them?

"I fear I've brought trouble upon us."

Chapter Nine

Pennsylvania Canal System Railroad
Central Pennsylvania

"Tell it again, David." If Lettie could hear more about the Englishmen then maybe it would assuage her fear. Terror still carried images of bounty hunters waiting for them at the end of this long journey by railroad and canal across this large and mountainous state.

Beneida squeezed her sweetheart's arm as the train rumbled over the tracks. "Yes, tell us again."

Nathan rolled his eyes. "I could likely tell it for him by now—he's repeated it so many times."

Lettie laughed. "Then do tell."

Seated across from her, David Bryant grinned. "When I sent you out the tavern's back door and on to the railroad by yourselves, the two men following us had just entered the tavern. I asked them to sit with me and told the waiter to have your lunches placed in tins."

Nathan patted his midsection. "Of course, you'd think of your victuals, David."

"I was only thinking of the three of you." The captain winked.

"And nearly missed the train!" Beneida swatted at his knee.

"But I didn't, did I?" David kissed her cheek. "Anyway, I detained them there and demanded that they tell me why they were following us."

"I can't believe they'd just sit there with you." Beneida cocked her head at him.

Lettie frowned. "How did you convince them? You've left that part out."

The captain patted at a lump in his coat pocket. "I have a friendly implement that helps on such occasions."

"A gun?" Beneida's eyes widened.

"I'm not sure they would have listened otherwise." The captain quirked his eyebrows.

"I can't imagine those men chasing across the ocean for Beneida." Would Nathan ever care for Lettie like that? Was he already falling in love with her? He'd never said so.

Nathan gazed at her with an intensity that made her cheeks heat. "He was besotted beyond all reason."

"I believe it was more lust, than love, that motivated Lord Wrenwick to pursue my beloved." David frowned. "Or I might be without a bride."

All that—sending men to find Beneida and bring her back to England—merely to be the man's mistress. How was that any different from being sold by one's master into sexual slavery?

Beneida's face flushed. "Even if Wrenwick offered marriage, I'd not have accepted."

"And who's to say those two gents would truly have conducted you back to England, had you agreed to be set up as the Englishman's mistress?" Nathan expressed a worry that Lettie, too, had considered herself.

What if those men had brought her friend back to Virginia and into a life of slavery again? Or took her to the brothels in New Orleans to descend to something worse than hell?

Lettie shivered.

Nathan took her hand. "You're cold."

"I warned you that rail and boat travel might make us miserably cold for some time." The captain sounded peevish.

Nathan settled his wool lap blanket around Lettie first and then himself. "Better?"

The warmth of the covering was nothing compared to the light in his eyes. That look said that he may love her. And she could no more part with Nathan when they arrived in Buffalo than she could survive without the very heart that beat in her chest.

But was his affection genuine?

Patriots' Inn
Northern Pennsylvania

Outside Lettie's second-story window, water dripped from icicles hanging two-feet long from the eaves of the inn's roofline. If freedom felt this frigid cold, could Lettie stand it? Yet, a little song bubbled up from within her heart: "Blest Be the Tie That Binds." Just like in the song, she, Beneida, Nathan, and David were bound together on this journey, bearing one another's burdens and woes. That morning, they'd all attended church services, where with one voice they'd sung the verses of the beautiful song. No wearing veils, no one pursuing them, simply a celebration of living life.

"Ready for lunch?" Beneida lifted a long ebony curl from her neck and pushed it back. Her rose-and-yellow-plaid day gown flattered her coloring. "No disrespect to your mother, but I was ready to be out of mourning clothes many miles ago."

Lettie gave a curt laugh. "Slaves don't have the privilege of mourning. And clothing in a certain color doesn't tell how I'm feeling inside." Surprisingly, she'd felt her mother's presence, not in a physical way but in her heart—Mama would have been overjoyed that Lettie had made it to freedom.

Beneida grabbed the key from the vanity table. The two went outside the small square room, and her friend locked the door behind them. She slid the ornate key into her reticule. "This is an old place."

"From the American Revolution." A war for independence, but not for all.

As they descended the stairs, the sweet scent of vanilla and cloves mingled with roast beef and yeasty bread. "Sure smells good."

"Um-hum, we haven't eaten this well in days on this part of the trip." Beneida patted her middle.

Without the padding, and with their rations being sparse, her friend looked like she was wasting away. But had her new friend been left at Burwell Plantation, she'd no doubt have become a very sorry sight.

Both Nathan and David rose when the two women arrived in the dining room downstairs. Only about sixteen paces in either direction square, the room held a surprising number of guests—at least two dozen people were seated at the tables.

"Letitia?" Nathan pulled back her rush-seated chair, and David did the same for her friend.

Beneida made a show of sniffing the air. "If it isn't roast beef, I may die."

"Maybe you should take up work onstage," David muttered. "You're sounding rather theatrical."

Nathan stifled a chuckle, as did Lettie.

At a nearby table sat a ginger-haired man attired in a navy brocade vest spattered with mustard-yellow dots and contrasting brown pants with a seam ribbon of tan. He peered over his newspaper at his companion, a tiny woman wearing clothing as drab, yet refined, as the man's was garish. "My dear, they are yet driving that law through— the Fugitive Slave Act."

The woman sniffed. "It's all botheration."

"Indeed." He leaned in on his elbows and folded the paper down. "Why do the denizens of our fine state need to have the federal government dictating what we are to do about those so fortunate as to escape their plight?"

So this man was sympathetic. Lettie's face warmed.

A man at an adjacent table, whose sparse, mouse-brown hair was plastered across his balding pate, cleared his throat, catching the other man's eye. "Why do you care if those Southerners willing to track down their property do so?"

Around them, a few ladies' eyes widened, and Lettie stared, too.

Nathan glared at the man.

The ginger-haired stranger stopped slicing his roast beef. "Sir, you forget yourself. You are in Pennsylvania—not in Georgia or Mississippi."

Nathan leaned toward her and whispered. "Pennsylvanians have enacted all kinds of statutes to prevent slaves from being returned."

The balding man stood, pulled off his gravy-stained napkin from his neck, and placed a fist on his narrow hip. "Soon, Pennsylvanians will be forced by federal law to comply with the return of property or they shall pay the price. You'll obey the law or face the consequences."

Property. That's how this man saw people like Lettie and Beneida.

David and Nathan shot to their feet, both with hands fisted.

Around them, other men rose from their tables and made shooing motions toward the horrid man. "Be off with you!"

"Go!" a chorus of voices arose.

Grabbing his coat and hat from a peg, the awful man soon scurried out to the hisses of the others. Lettie's heart beat hard in her chest.

Nathan's nostrils flared as he and David both sat back down.

"Pray God they don't push that bill through." Nathan took her hand in his and squeezed it gently.

"They won't," the captain insisted.

What if they did? Would these brave men be willing to leave their country behind? Did she and Beneida have the right to ask them to do so?

No. We have no rights.

So if it came to that, she and Beneida could travel to Canada. Alone.

Chapter Ten

Erie Canal
Northern New York

Nathan couldn't stop beaming. Despite the cholera outbreak in New York, they've not yet encountered any problems. And his beloved was now free. He'd not let fear squash his joy down.

"Next stop is the inn, folks." The canal man called out from the front. "Be gathering up your belongings—and your children and pets."

Letitia gazed out at the verdant landscape. "It's so beautiful here."

He grasped her hand. "And you're free."

Her smile was the finest thing he'd ever seen.

She dipped her chin. "I don't know what we'd have done without you and Captain Bryant."

Nathan longed to pull her into his arms and kiss her right there in front of everyone.

David pointed ahead as a long low building came into view set back from the shoreline. With unpainted wood walls, it more resembled a rambling shack than an inn.

"That can't be it." Nathan scowled. The slaves at most James River plantations resided in similar structures, albeit smaller.

"If I were a gambling man, I'd place a full dollar on that being our night's stay."

Beneida chuckled. "Gonna be funny if it is, 'cause I can't picture all these white folks beddin' down in that place."

"Stop ahead!" The canal man called out.

Nathan exchanged a look with David. "Maybe there's something further back?"

"Mama, we aren't staying in that old place, are we?" A tousle-haired boy squeezed his disheveled mother's arm.

"Hush, boy. It's only for the night." She patted the boy's tawny head and the man beside her, presumably her husband, swore.

Nervous voices carried around them.

"This ain't nothin' compared to what we've slept in, is it, Lettie?" Beneida winked at Letitia.

Nathan rolled his eyes heavenward. *Lord, get us safely to our destination and be with us this evening.*

"They'll not put us up someplace that isn't safe." David puffed out his chest but the look on his face belied his words.

Soon they'd been secured to the side of the canal and the passengers had disembarked. Two by two they walked over the well-trod dirt path that led to the spartan building.

The door opened and a heavyset man stepped outside, a pipe in his hands. "Welcome, travelers!"

"Hope he puts that pipe out well before he lays his head down at night," Nathan grumbled to his friend.

"No doubt."

They followed the others into the building, which was an open, long, rectangular space covered with low cots. The only partition was a string of dingy gray wool blankets that divided the room.

"Men over here." The proprietor pointed to his left and then to his right. "And ladies and children over there."

"Not exactly ideal." David's laugh was definitely a nervous one.

His confident friend was rarely rattled, but this place had the same effect upon Nathan.

Letitia turned and took his hands. "We'll be all right here. Don't you worry."

They'd not be sleeping that night. No doubt he and David would be awake, keeping watch over their ladies.

"There's fireplaces at both ends and the cots have both pillows and blankets." Beneida smiled at David. "Luxury."

"You're right." His friend's shoulders relaxed.

"And there were bunches of outhouses right off in the woods." Letitia raised her eyebrows. "So, this must be a mighty fine accommodation."

Nathan huffed a laugh. "There's a pump right out front for water, too."

Letitia pointed to the wall. "Free."

The sign on the wall read, *Free cold water, hot water for washing one cent*. But from the tears pooling in his sweetheart's eyes, that wasn't what she meant. And he wasn't sure if she'd been able to read the rest of the words. With the pads of his thumbs, he wiped the tears to keep them from spilling down her cheeks.

"Free."

Beneida sat down beside Lettie on her cot. "Those two men, they're fine ones."

Her heart knew one thing but her head, or was it fear, called out something else.

"You gonna marry him if he ask?" Beneida patted Lettie's hand and she pulled it away.

"Ain't no one gonna take care of me if I can take care of my own self." Now why had she spoken those petulant words?

Clucking her tongue, her friend rose. "You best be thinkin' of what the Lord would have you do—not what Miss Lettie fears she must do."

Discomfort coursed through Lettie. When she closed her eyes at night, she could see white men beating her mother. Mama lying there, the lifeblood draining from her. And nothing Lettie could do. She swallowed hard, remembering what Mama had cautioned her. "Don't be trustin' no white man, Lettie. You sets yourself on your own two feet if'n you get free."

She exhaled the breath she'd been holding.

Women in the far corner tried to soothe fretting children. One baby wouldn't stop crying.

"I'm going outside away from that noise." Beneida huffed and then strode off.

The wails persisted and Lettie rose from her cot and approached the mother and child. She'd never have dared to do such a thing as a slave. She'd been taught that she wasn't equal to white people. That she was nothing. Worse than nothing. Still, she continued forward to where the woman paced, babe in arms.

Dark circles beneath the woman's eyes spoke of sleepless nights. The proprietor had brought a caned rocker to the corner for the woman to rock the child, but rocking hadn't helped.

Letitia moved toward the frazzled mother and extended her arms. "I'll be right here with your baby." She bit her lower lip. She'd felt that she'd had to explain that she wouldn't run off with the child. Why would the stranger even have thought such a thing? Because maybe she sensed Lettie was a runaway slave.

Be still and know I am God.

Lettie shivered.

The woman's blue eyes widened. Had she heard the voice that had spoken to Lettie's soul? *No. Not possible.* But the mother handed over the squirming bundle and Lettie pulled the tiny babe, who felt not much more than a newborn, to her shoulder. Then she paced the floor slowly, rubbing the infant's warm back. The wails softened to small cries. The child's mother sank down onto a nearby cot.

Lettie kept walking, up to the blanketed wall and back to the rocking chair. The baby stopped crying but pulled its tiny legs up once in a while and would gurgle out a tiny sob. She sat in the chair and situated the babe on her lap. Who would bring a newborn on such a journey? A desperate woman. Wasn't Lettie also on such a journey? She was free now.

Joy coursed through her and she sang to the child. She rubbed the baby's cheek and it rooted, grasping onto her index finger. She stifled a cry when a tooth bit into her flesh. This was no newborn. This was a hungry and underfed baby. She unwrapped the cloths swaddling the baby. As she suspected, the infant was thin and its belly swollen.

"Excuse me?" One of the other mothers whispered to her as she approached.

"Yes?"

The dark-haired woman pointed to the front of her sleeping gown, with circular wet spots. "I think that babe isn't getting fed proper-like. And I've got plenty left to spare."

"It's not my baby."

"I know. I've watched the mother try to feed this wee one and I think the poor dear is dry." Dark brown eyes locked on Lettie. She pointed to where the mother lay, sound asleep on her cot. "Let me feed him or her now while I can."

Love's Escape

Lettie rose and handed the baby over. "I'll keep watch in case the mother awakes. Oh, and there's at least one tooth come up in that little mouth—so watch out."

The woman chuckled. Soon she rocked and fed the baby, who made such loud slurping sounds that Lettie became embarrassed. She sang a lullaby that her mother had taught her.

"I know that song," the other woman said, wiping tears from her eyes. "My mother sang that to me before they took her away."

"Oh no." Lettie rubbed her chill arms. "What happened?"

"They sold her."

Tears threatened. Lettie sniffed as the other woman closed her eyes. "I'm sorry."

"I thank God I'm free now."

"Me, too," Lettie whispered.

"You?" The woman's dark eyes widened.

Lettie nodded.

The babe finally ceased feeding and when placed on Lettie's shoulder emitted a hearty belch. The two women laughed. "I'm Mrs. Smith, and your secret is safe with me."

"As is yours." Lettie continued rubbing the now-full baby's back. "And may I tell you something?"

Pain, that had been bundled in her gut just as this baby's had been, roiled out of her.

"Yes'm, do."

Lettie sniffed. "Is your mother yet living?"

The woman beamed. "She is and my husband—he's a farmer in Buffalo—is working to have her freed, too."

"That's good." Lettie drew in a fortifying breath. "Mrs. Smith, while your mother was taken from you, she wasn't. . ." She shuddered. "She wasn't. . ." Shaking violently, she couldn't voice the words. The other woman hadn't experienced having her

107

mother murdered in front of a crowd of onlookers. So much evil in the world.

"Child, child, don't say it. I knows of what you speak." The woman's dialect slipped back into what it likely once had been. "Now you sit down there and rock. You a good woman. You stepped in when no one else in this place would help out. You gave me the push to offer something I had plenty to give. Just rest."

Lettie sniffed. She nodded as hot tears warmed her face.

"You and me, we're free now. Free. Free to choose to help or not. And you made the better choice, Missy, just now."

Free. What a wonderful word.

And she could make her own decisions.

Would her choices include Nathan?

Chapter Eleven

Buffalo, New York

Nathan stood and stretched as the canal boat came to a full stop. The workers scrambled to secure it. His muscles ached and head throbbed. "Ships, trains, canal boats, stagecoach—I think the only thing we've missed out on is horseback."

The canal man strolled through, grinning. "Buffalo, folks."

Nathan stroked his thick reddish beard while David scratched his more pepper than salt, goatee.

"Stop doing that," Beneida hissed at his friend as David helped her from her seat. With light powder, a mole near her eye and one on her chin, and her eyebrows broadened and darker, she wasn't the stunning woman she normally was.

Letitia her curls covered with some sort of turban-looking wrap, stood with shoulders squared. "It's mighty pretty here. I can say that!"

Tall oak and maple trees were covered in new leaf. Narcissus, serviceberry, and flowering plum trees covered the park near the canal's wharf. On their way in, they'd viewed farm fields freshly tilled and edged by thick towering pines. New construction of homes and businesses bespoke the area's prosperity.

Nathan pointed to Letitia's feet, which were shoved into some tight, high-heeled satin pumps. "Those won't last more than a half mile if we must walk."

She looked down her nose, the low-cut bodice of her gown revealed she was more amply endowed than he'd imagined. The half-dozen gaudy necklaces strung around her long neck dangled into her cleavage, drawing the eye there.

Beneida had insisted, at the last stop, that this getup would be perfect. Still, Nathan felt uncomfortable seeing Lettie attired in what he considered to be more appropriate for a trollop. Still, she had a point that if the Englishmen hadn't been deterred then they may have followed them to New York. Hence the men had also allowed their beards to fill in.

David pulled his watch from his vest pocket and examined it. "I'd like to run down to the port, if you don't mind. I want to check on the position I telegrammed them about."

"You go ahead, then." Nathan inclined his head toward the departing travelers. "I'll get the luggage, and we'll go on to the hotel."

"Are you sure?"

"Yes. Now go." Nathan and the ladies lingered in their spot, allowing David to move into the crush of people departing. "I hope there are taxis around when we get out."

Within the hour, they'd retrieved their belongings and had been brought by carriage to their hotel, not far from the wharf but in a questionable part of town. Were David's funds running so low? He'd been the one to make the arrangements and hadn't said anything about there being a problem. Now that they were in port, perhaps Nathan should take a chance and wire Father.

Thankfully, the rooms were immediately adjacent one another, so Nathan could listen for any signs of trouble for the women. He quickly unpacked his satchel and then washed. Were

Love's Escape

they all really here? His head felt clogged with cotton bolls. He laid down on the bed to take a quick nap.

A loud rap roused Nathan from slumber. Where was he? He tossed aside the thin covering and rose, the bedsprings creaking.

"Nate, it's me."

He pulled his suspenders over his shoulders and went to the door and opened it. "I fell asleep."

David strode in, his eyes red as though he'd been crying, and slumped into a ladder-back oak chair by the wall. "They have no positions for me."

"Nothing?"

"No."

"What?" Nathan shoved a hand back through his hair.

His friend shook his head. "I can't believe it."

Neither could Nathan.

"I was counting on this—that there would be a shipping job." David paced. "And there is none."

"No work?"

Had she heard right? Lettie pressed her ear to the thin wall.

Nathan's fragmented voice carried in fits and spurts. "How. . .support. . .all? Cash. . .that tight?"

"Someone will hire." David Bryant's bass voice held false confidence.

"I can. . .work. . .Great Lakes."

Nathan had been so ill aboard the ship, how could he be employed on a boat? He'd be too seasick to work.

The two men's voices lowered, and Lettie could no longer understand them. A knock at the door startled her. But then the key rattled in the lock. "I've got the water," Beneida called as she opened the door. She carried in a half-full pitcher.

111

Lettie took the water from her and set it on the wobbly washstand. "We need to go ahead with our own plan."

"To support ourselves?"

"Yes."

Beneida slumped onto the bed, the springs creaking loudly. "Where?"

"Wherever we can get work." And she needed to save enough money for if and when Congress passed that wretched law. She would leave for Canada while Nathan could remain in his own country. To return to his family in Virginia and resume helping others to freedom. But how could she go on without him at her side?

Somehow, she'd have to. If work was hard to come by here, how much more so in Canada? Abolitionists might be sympathetic to Lettie and Beneida's plights, but would they really put themselves out to help two white Southern men?

Tomorrow she'd get up and find whatever work was available. She was no stranger to toil. But she was free. And if freedom meant working sunup to sundown with no master owning her, she'd not complain.

She'd *do*.

Just like Mama had taught her.

Both Nathan and David had slept through much of their second day in Buffalo, much to their chagrin. At dinner the previous night, their only meal of the day, Nathan and his friend had apologized to the women, who both seemed very subdued. Neither he nor David had been able to get the ladies to share their concerns, nor what they'd been doing that day.

Now, Nathan pushed through his morning ablutions, readying for the day.

Love's Escape

Determined to get to the docks at first light, he dressed with the aid of the flickering single oil lamp. Then he tucked a hard roll in his pocket and headed out.

Street sweepers, carters, women selling muffins from piled-high baskets, and maids attired in stark black-and-white uniforms populated the walkway. As he neared the dock, he passed groups of fishermen and uniformed boatmen who smoked pipes outside the boatyard.

Nathan smiled and nodded to a well-dressed man whose dark hair and eyes, combined with golden skin, suggested he was at least partly of Native American descent. The stranger carried stacks of boxes.

"Are those filled with paperwork?" Nathan inquired.

"Yes."

Not long ago, although it seemed ages with their escape, Nathan had been hunched over a desk managing Father's ledgers. Such was his occupation. Now, though, he'd take any work he could get, including deckhand even if his constitution rebelled. "Can you direct me to the hiring office for the Blue Star Line?"

"They have an office dockside in that building there." The tall man, wearing a navy suit, inclined his head toward a long, shingled building adjacent to the water. "I'm heading that way, so join me."

"Thanks." Something about the man, who was perhaps five years older than himself, seemed familiar. His voice, too, was reminiscent of another man.

"Where're you from?" The man shifted his load, which looked heavy.

"Virginia. And I'd be glad to help you with one of those boxes." Nathan extended his hands.

The stranger passed Nathan a sturdy box, which weighed about ten pounds. "Normally they wouldn't bother me, but I've been moving our office from across town a little at a time."

They fell into step beside each other. "Where do you work?"

"At the ferry to Canada."

"Do you like it?"

The man laughed. "I can't wait until they put me back on the water again."

"I think my friend David feels that way, but his promised captain's position was gone when we arrived."

"So you're new here?"

"Yes."

"And your pal can't sail?"

"Right."

"What about you? Were you a Virginia waterman?"

"No. Not sure I have boat legs." Nathan didn't normally share that he was a funeral home clerk. "I'm an office worker and happy to tally numbers."

The other man chuckled, a sound so deep in his chest that it rumbled, again recalling another gentleman. *Someone kind.*

"You should talk with the stevedore's manager, then. Wellington is looking for someone."

"Certainly." Nathan had nothing to lose. Unless he was required to frequently be aboard a ship. "What does a stevedore do?"

Again, the ferryman laughed. "The stevedores haul stuff on and off the ships. But the manager tracks those materials. And the men. Some of whom can be, well, a trifle. . ."

Nathan gave a curt laugh. "I think I understand." He'd observed the workers at Richmond's docks. Granted some of their cargos included people. Treated no better than animals. Worse even.

Love's Escape

The man turned his head toward Nathan and smiled, his large white teeth gleaming against his tan skin. "One must be wise in the ways of the world to manage those stevedores."

As if to illustrate his point, a group of men ahead began pushing one another and cursing loudly. Then one spit a stream of tobacco so close to them, they had to quickstep back to avoid being hit.

"As I was saying. . ." The man shook his head, a dark curly lock falling against his forehead in the same way Nathan's often did.

Letitia would push Nathan's sandy-red curls back in a gesture that was quickly becoming familiar and heartfelt. If he could land a job. If they could get settled. What would life be like as her husband? His neck heated at his errant thought.

Soon they neared the dock and the whitewashed building. "This way."

Nathan followed the man into the building. Removing his hat, he ducked beneath the low entryway and went inside, hat in hand, box in the other.

Large windows dominated the left wall, which allowed light to stream into the long hallway that fronted the offices. Cigar and pipe smoke formed a gray cloud that was barely diminished with the opening of the entry door. Sturdy oak chairs were occupied by men whose attire ranged from that of dockhands to the more refined businessmen wearing suits, loose ties, and shoes buffed to a shine.

The stranger paused by an open door and rapped on the frame, grinning at whoever sat inside. "Have you got a moment, Mr. Wellington?"

"Certainly," a deep voice boomed from inside. "Always time for you, Marrton." The man's thick Scottish brogue drew out Nathan's companion's name.

When motioned forward, Nathan stepped into the room. A glass-fronted filing cabinet to the right was crammed so full that the brass fastener looked as though it might pop free. The narrow oak desk had three piles of paper in stacks and a spindle half full. To the left were two wide-seated Windsor chairs, covered with boxes. The man behind the desk rose. He stood close to their height, with a head of hair almost as dark as David's and nearly as wavy. His dark blue eyes reminded Nathan of deep ocean waters, but his broad smile immediately put him at ease.

"I'd ask you gentlemen to sit, but as you can see. . ." He pointed to the clutter surrounding him, "I'm in the midst of a pile of paperwork."

A box marked "Bills of lading" teetered at the edge of the desk, and Nathan was sorely tempted to push it back.

"Did your assistant quit, then, Welly?"

Wellington exhaled loudly. "He did. But I'm sure that's not the reason that you're here, Marty."

"No, indeed. I met this man on the way in." Marrton quirked his eyebrows. "And he has office experience."

Nathan stepped forward and extended his arm in a manner that wouldn't topple the piles. "Nathan Pleasant, sir."

"Good to meet you." He extended a broad hand. Mr. Wellington possessed a grip so strong that Nathan fought the urge to wince.

Beside him, he sensed Mr. Marrton shifting his weight. Probably needed to leave. Instead, the dark-haired man removed the boxes from one of the chairs and settled into it, as though planning to stay. Finally, Wellington released Nathan's hand.

Framed documents and certificates dominated the wall behind the agent. A newspaper clipping, peeking from the edge of the man's papers, had the bold headline "Another freighter sunk outside Milwaukee." Apprehension chipped away at Nathan's

Love's Escape

resolve to take whatever work he could. But he had Letitia to think of and their future together.

"Sir, you say you require an assistant?"

"I do. And you performed accounting and general paperwork elsewhere?"

"Yes. In Virginia."

"That's wonderful news to me, Mr. Pleasant."

"I'm glad, sir."

The shipping agent rubbed his cleft chin and aimed his gaze at Marrton. "The Frenchmen and métis in these parts, like you Marrton, would pronounce this man's name as Plez-awnt." Wellington accented the second syllable instead of the first.

"Yes. *Plaisante* is how my mother's tribe pronounced my English name, which is Pleasant." His tone turned clipped.

Marrton—was that pronunciation meant to be *Martin*?

Like Father.

Wellington glanced between them. "Do you have family in these parts, Nathan?"

He cleared his throat, suddenly uncomfortable. "Thirty-eight years ago, my father fought in the War of 1812, after rebelliously running away from home to join the navy." Shivers coursed through him with growing recognition.

"His name?" The ferryman's deep voice commanded the same attention Father's always had.

"Martin Pleasant."

"Martin Pleasant, *Senior*?" With Father's same mannerism of tugging at his tie when stressed, the man stood and drew in a heavy breath.

Nathan stared, recognizing the truth. "He looked for you for so long." So very long, until Father had finally given up. Chills continued down his arms. Dampness threatened his eyes.

"He left me behind."

"He had to." Nathan splayed his hands. The tribe had insisted.

Mr. Wellington came around the side of the desk and clapped Martin on his shoulder. "My friend, thank you for bringing Nathan to me. You may continue this family conversation when I'm done with our interview, *ye ken*?"

Nathan's half-brother nodded curtly. Would he come back? From the angry look on his face, likely not. Martin spun on his heel and departed.

Wellington's eyebrows rose nearly as high as the fringe of bangs that bobbed on his forehead. "Well, that was interesting, but not what either of us needs to address at this moment. Sit down and tell me about your skills."

"Yes, sir."

The whole time they talked, Nathan's mind kept wandering to the chance encounter he'd had that had brought him full circle from where his father had begun. Father had headed as far North as he could to get away from his own controlling father. And away from Richmond. But when Father's Chippewa wife had died, in Michigan, her tribe had insisted he leave his son with them. Would his half-brother believe him?

Did Martin even know what had happened?

Clearly not.

Martin's mother, and Father's love for her, had resulted in Nathan's being schooled that all people were created equally. That no one race was better than another.

Now Nathan had found Father's firstborn son.

He'd not let Father down.

Chapter Twelve

Like the rushing water of the Niagara Falls, the week had burst past, with each of them heading out in a different direction each morning after a quick breakfast downstairs. Lettie alone sat by the window, sipping her dark coffee, savoring the quiet moments. She possessed the luxury of leaving last, for her work at the new hat shop just down the street. Nathan and David headed off to the wharves first, followed by Beneida, who'd found a position at a dressmaker's shop.

God had brought her out of slavery. But a glance at the *Buffalo Journal*'s headline announced just how tenuous her situation was—"COMPROMISE GAINS SUPPORT."

What kind of compromise was it to penalize people a thousand dollars for aiding enslaved people to freedom and then returning the "property" to owners?

Rise up, girl. Mama would have told her to rise and let God's light shine through her. Lettie hadn't really understood that until recently.

She lowered her head and closed her eyes. *God, I'm trusting You. You know I want to be free.* She'd always feel chased unless the Lord lifted this burden.

"Miss Lettie?"

She looked up at the maid, whose beautiful bronze skin reminded her so much of Mama's. "Yes?"

The young woman fished a cream-colored envelope out of her pocket and handed it to Lettie. "This be for you, miss."

"Thank you." She accepted it and laid it atop the blue gingham tablecloth before opening the missive. She recognized that it was from her grandfather, with *Parkes* scrawled across the back of the envelope. Could her limited reading skills allow her to read it? She sounded out the top section slowly. *Dearest Lettie, My grand...*

"Lettie!" Beneida swooped in to join Letitia at her table, eyes wide. "I wasn't expecting you here."

"I have a letter."

"Yes, and David received a telegram, and I suspect Nathan may have gotten something, too. We sent an errand boy to him at the wharf to see."

Face pale, Beneida pressed a palm to her chest and sank into the chair beside Lettie. "We're to be married this afternoon, and David will try to be transferred to the Canadian line."

"What?" Lettie sat up straight, her heart pounding.

"We think Nathan's half-brother, Martin, contacted his father by telegram. Mr. Pleasant, in turn, went to David's father. So, if Burwell discovered where we are, if some busybody passed on Martin's information, then we may be in danger."

Lettie stared, gape-mouthed.

"Might not be those Englishmen, alone, that we need to watch for, Lettie." Beneida began opening the drawers. "David sent me a message to go and get ready."

Lettie could scarcely breathe. "I'll go to Canada, then, as I planned."

"What does your letter say?"

Lettie pushed the missive to her friend. "Would you read it?"

"Certainly." Beneida quickly scanned the letter.

"I meant read it aloud to me, please."

Smiling, Beneida turned to her, eyes filled with happy tears. "You're free! Your grandfather purchased your contract."

Love's Escape

She sucked in a breath, scarce able to believe her friend's words. "How?"

"Master Burwell was *convinced* by your grandfather's gun." Beneida's eyebrows rose.

Lettie gasped. "Did he shoot him?"

Laughing, Beneida pointed to the middle of the page. "He says he opted to let the miscreant live but made Burwell sign over a bill of sale for you."

"Oh, Lord, have mercy. . ." A shudder of relief course through her down to her laced-up work boots.

"He adds, however, that the slave broker, Cheney, has gone missing." She looked up. "And that the overseer, Durham, met his end in a way old Mr. Parkes would not wish upon anyone."

"Oh, my. Was it Satilde?"

"Maybe so, because he says Cheney was transporting Satilde to Richmond, for sale, but neither made it there."

The two locked gazes and then sat silently for a moment.

Lettie shivered. "There will always be more Cheneys and Durhams out there to replace those wicked men."

"But there are good men like our men and Mr. Parkes." Beneida smiled. "He promises to send your freedom papers by special courier and is having copies made."

Free. "I can hardly believe it!" And Nathan would be at liberty to marry whomever he pleased. He'd not have to feel bound to protect her anymore.

Why did that make her sad?

"It's true. Says so right here."

Lettie sniffed back tears. "But, Beneida, what about you?"

"Let me finish reading and see if he says." She bent over the letter and quickly moved from the first to second page. Her expression changed from one of awe, to confusion, to sadness.

"Mr. Parkes just says Burwell told him that Lord Wrenwick would be happy with me and to not concern himself."

"Oh, Beneida, Mr. Burwell must have known about Wrenwick's two men pursuing you, then."

"Probably aided them."

"No doubt."

"It's all right." Her friend brushed moisture from her eyes. "David and I will marry and get on with our new life."

"But you'll be gone to Canada. And sailing on the Great Lakes."

"Yes."

Lettie, too, would need to be gone as soon as her papers arrived. But, oh, how her heart would grieve her loss of her friends.

And of the man she loved.

By the time Mr. Wellington could release him from work, Nathan had himself worked up to give his brother, Martin, an earful. Hadn't the man even thought of what his careless telegram could have wrought?

"Mr. Pleasant?" The dirty street waif that he'd sent to the inn with a message, stood in the doorway. "Do I still get my money even if I couldn't find 'em?"

Had they already gone? David may have panicked and run. "Did you stop at the millinery shop?"

"Yes, sir, but they said Lettie had drawn her wages and left."

"Left?"

"Yes, sir." The boy held out his grimy hand and David placed several coins there. With wide eyes, he counted the amount aloud and grinned. "Thanks!" He sped out of the building, brushing past Wellington as he went.

Love's Escape

Nathan rushed to the inn. Where would Lettie have gone? Was she in hiding? They'd agreed to meet at the church they were attending.

Surely Pastor Maher or his wife would know. And what of Beneida and David? Would they still marry when they learned that she was free—that Miss Dolley should have been free all along? Amazing what evil that money slipped into the pocket of a greedy judge would do.

Father had included a clip from the *Richmond Times* with his letter to Nathan, that explained how Lord Wrenwick had arrived in town in high dudgeon and had pursued the matter until Mr. Dolley's will was produced and legal documents clearly showed Beneida should have been freed upon his death. How would David react if Beneida now refused to marry him? Would the ebony-haired beauty no longer need his friend once her freedom was secure?

Apparently Lettie had thought so. She was gone. Without a word to him.

Once inside the hotel building, he clattered up the stairs to their rooms. No one answered at either door. He unlocked his room. All of David's belongings were gone. Inside Letitia's room, a maid was dusting the bare room.

"They at church, sir."

"Thank you." They were at church, but all their belongings were packed. Would they have already gone on?

Nathan exited the building and hurried down the street, dodging pedestrians. When he arrived at the Church of Eternal Salvation, an abolitionist meeting place, he tried the sanctuary door.

Locked.

He knocked.

No one answered.

He pounded harder.

A metallic clicking sounded as someone inside unlocked the door and pushed it open. Mrs. Maher, a pretty blond woman about Letitia's height, placed a finger by her lips. "We have a wedding going on here."

In the front, Pastor Maher held his Bible and spoke to Beneida and David.

Where was Letitia? He scanned the square sanctuary, all ten rows of benches empty.

"Would you like to witness with me?" Mrs. Maher asked softly.

"Where's Letitia?"

At the ferry, Lettie sought out Martin Pleasant. She spied a man of Nathan's height and similar build, his back turned to her, attired in a dove-gray long coat and matching trousers, and a top hat. When he turned, Lettie couldn't suppress her surprise and gave a little gasp. The man resembled an image of Nathan but dipped in caramel. This had to be his half-brother.

Nathan had met with Martin once, and had shared about their past, but hadn't seen him again. While she was grateful his telegram had helped her grandfather find her, he may have imperiled her friend.

She strode toward the man. "Mr. Pleasant?"

He tipped his tall hat. "May I help you?"

"I'm Lettie, Nathan's. . ." What was she to him? His friend?

"His fiancée?" Martin grinned broadly, revealing large white teeth. "No wonder he fell so deeply in love with you."

Lettie couldn't manage a response. Her heart sputtered in fits and starts. Was that really what Nathan had told him?

"Glad to meet you, Letitia. And happy for what little part I may have had in bringing you two together, or possibly my grandmother's influence."

She frowned. "What do you mean?"

"My father, too, married the descendant of a slave—in his case, a Sioux maiden captured and given to a French lieutenant at Fort Mackinac." He rubbed his chin. "When the English came in, my grandmother escaped with my mother and obtained work at Fort Detroit. That's where my father, and Nathan's, met her."

"I see."

"Nathan told me that our father shared this history with him as the reason that drove him to support abolitionist work in the South. He'd seen firsthand how slavery had affected my mother and grandmother."

She felt a strange kinship to this man. An understanding. "I thank you for sharing. But I'm here for help."

"In any way." He extended his hands as passengers, carrying satchels, streamed toward the wharf and the ferries.

"You see, your telegram to Mr. Pleasant may have alerted slave catchers to our location."

He pressed his dark eyes closed. "I wasn't thinking. I was just so anxious to contact him."

"Yes, well some good came of that, for me." The wind rustled her skirts and the loose trim of her bonnet. She cupped her hand to hold the flapping fabric, leaning in as though in confidence. "But my friend may be at risk."

"I'm so sorry. Tell me what you need."

Their carriage stopped by the Blue Star Line Ferry, and they got out, Nathan first.

David paid the driver and grinned at Nathan. "My father's a gem. He transferred funds for me, and now we won't have to worry. Nor live in that squalid inn."

Nathan scanned the queue of passengers but didn't spy Letitia.

"There she is!" Beneida waved, jumping up and down like a child.

"My darling, we're in public."

But Beneida ignored David and ran off ahead of them.

"No doubt happy to share her news." David sighed. "Let's hope Lettie likes your idea."

His neck suddenly hot, Nathan loosened his cravat. If all went well, tonight he'd have a bride.

"Come on, Nate." David darted ahead, dodging through the line.

"Excuse me," Nathan repeated over and over again as he weaved through the groups of passengers, in pursuit of his friend and on to his future wife. If she'd have him.

When he finally reached her, Letitia and Beneida were hugging and crying. David stood behind them, arms crossed. From a small, whitewashed building to the right, Martin emerged, holding up what looked like tickets.

Nathan inched closer to Letitia, waiting for his moment.

"Who's going to Canada?" Martin asked.

Letitia glanced from his brother to him, a question in her eyes.

Nathan swooped upon Lettie like a bird of prey. He wrapped his arms possessively around her and kissed her so soundly that Lettie could scarcely breathe. The dock seemed to fade away, the passengers' voices dimming, as she sank into the warmth of his promise. His lips covered hers and then moved to her cheek and then close to her ear.

Her breath stuttered.

"Will you have me as your husband, even though you are free to choose whoever you want?" Nathan's lips traveled up her cheek to her mouth again before she could respond. Then he embraced her and held her so tenderly that she buried her face in his jacket, wanting the moment to never end.

David cleared his throat. "I think we'd better get them back to the church before Pastor and Mrs. Maher get busy with tonight's meeting."

"And before they make any more of a spectacle of themselves on my wharf." Martin harrumphed.

Lettie broke free from Nathan's grasp. "Sorry." Face flushed, she tried to straighten her cap, which had been knocked askew.

"I'm not sorry." Nathan grabbed her hand. "I love you and want you to be my wife."

"I love you, too." She closed her eyes and tipped her head back and was rewarded with another delicious kiss.

"We don't have the licenses yet, but we do have a church, a pastor, and can be your witnesses." Beneida's face glowed.

"And we're free."

Nathan turned to face his brother. "I don't think we'll be needing that ferry ride to Canada, now that both have their papers coming. Thank you for your unintended wedding gift."

"Anytime. And a ride on the ferry just for fun is yours for the asking." Martin winked at him. "Several nice private inns over there, on the other side of the water."

"We'll be back in an hour, then, after we see the preacher." Nathan laughed.

Heat crept into Lettie's face. "I don't think I agreed to anything yet."

"Will you say your vows?"

"If you'll say yours." She locked gazes with him, suddenly feeling shy.

"I'll see you back later, then." Martin wrapped an arm around Nathan and around Lettie. "I'll send word for a cottage to be held for you on the other side tonight."

The other side.

The other side of slavery was freedom. She'd finally arrived in the promised land. And she didn't have to wait for heaven to be there.

She could indeed make her own decisions.

And she chose Nathan Pleasant—and a life with him.

The End

Author's Notes

The daffodil was being cultivated more widely in the Mid-Atlantic area at this time. There was no known symbol of the daffodil being used to identify "conductors"—I just made that up. And it's hard to believe that our Eastern seaboard wasn't highly populated. In 1850, our cities were the size of many of today's suburbs or smaller.

In the 1850 census, slaves were included on the household lists. I think of my heroine and her friend and can only imagine how horrible it would be to have one's name listed as property.

Train travel was taking off during this time. Likewise ship travel was changing drastically with the transition from sail-powered to engine-powered ships (steamboats). There were even hybrid ships, which were a combination of both. A great reference book you may want to read is *Wet Britches and Muddy Boots: A History of Travel in Victorian America* by John H. White Jr. (Indiana University Press, 2013).

As mentioned in the story, the Fugitive Slave Act of 1850 was part of the Compromise of 1850. During the Mexican-American War, as new territories were acquired, there was acrimony between slave owners in the South and abolitionists in the North. In addition, those who favored states' rights to enforcing or not enforcing the return of slaves didn't want the federal government to enforce the return of "property." Unfortunately, the new act made slavery a protected institution and set up the beginning of the buildup to our Civil War. As slave catchers swarmed the North and states fought back against legislation, abolitionist sentiment burgeoned. My hero and heroine live in a time on the cusp of tremendous turmoil.

Philadelphia was a hotbed of the abolitionist movement. William Still, a free-born Black man and one of Philly's most successful businessmen, was indeed an abolitionist during this time. And his wife, like my heroine, was named Letitia! The information about the Liberty Bell is correct. Even though we'd been there for previous research, my family and I even made a trip to Philadelphia in which we visited the bell and I got the lay of the land for this story. I'd never seen it before. If you get a chance—go visit!

Martin Pleasant, Junior, is fictional but there were many métis children who were returned to their Chippewa tribes if the mother died. There was good reason for this. One would be that the child could then grow up with the tribe's culture. The other was the concern that the father would place the child/children in orphanages away from the care of the tribe or in schools for Native American children where they would lose their heritage. I have an extended family member who had this happen to them, where the father put the children all in the orphanage. As far as Martin, Senior, not being able to find his son again, that's also highly likely that the tribe would keep that information from anyone (in particular, Caucasian men) who inquired.

There were many slaves who were supposed to be freed upon their masters' or mistresses' deaths and yet they were kept enslaved. Living in Virginia, I've heard these stories many times in the history of the Commonwealth and elsewhere. Corrupt judges could be swayed to ignore the wills. Evil exists today where people are kept enslaved against their will and others keep it covered up. Let's keep praying about that and do what we can to help.

We lived south of Buffalo for a while. Such a wonderful wealth of history there. Buffalo was indeed a spot for runaways to go, because then there was the possibility to cross into Canada.

Acknowledgments

To God—You know I couldn't do any of this without You. My husband and son, Jeffrey D. and Clark J. Pagels, for putting up with my writing life and supporting me in my efforts. Kathleen L. Maher, who is like an angel sent from God to help me with her amazing critique partnering, brainstorming, and fund of information! Kathy, an award-winning author, even critiqued the second version for me! Her generosity knows no bounds!

Thank you to my beta readers for the second edition: Tina St. Clair Rice who has been a longtime fantastic beta reader and friend and Jennifer Magers who is a newer wonderful beta reader and friend, to a new beta reader who stepped up to help—Emily Kowalski Smith. Thanks, also, to my *Love's Escape* Promo Team members for their help and the Pagels' Pals members for their support for my writing ministry!

Thank you to Julian Charity, Shirley Plantation's former historian, for sharing with me about slaves being smuggled out of some plantations via caskets. Much appreciation to my friends, Libbie and Mack Cornett, for discussing her family's funeral home business with me and about the history of the Shockoe area in Richmond. Libbie introduced me to Christian fiction back when we were both new mothers in Charleston, South Carolina.

Thank you to my mother-in-law, Joan Pagels, for help with corrections on the original story, during a very difficult time. God bless the 1K1HR Facebook Group members for support and encouragement, particularly Deb Garland.

This story was originally published as a much shorter novella in *The Captive Brides* collection with Barbour Publishing. Thank you to Rebecca Germany for this collection's seminal idea, to Cynthia Hickey inviting me to join in with that group effort, and to my editor, Becky Durost Fish. Thank you, also, to Laura Young, who is always such a blessing.

Book Club Questions

1. Were you brought up somewhere that included instruction about the Underground Railroad and about abolition movements?
2. Where does God fit into all that movement?
3. If you were alive during that time, do you think you'd have been brave enough to assist someone to freedom?
4. Nathan really loves Letitia and he wants her to make her own choices. When we give our own will over to the Lord, He blesses us. Have you ever set your ego aside, to ask God to make a situation like He plans it to go, not as how you wanted it to go? What happened then?
5. Beneida had expectations that she'd be freed but then she wasn't. Have you ever had someone let you down after they'd promised you something major? How did you feel? How did God heal that hurt?

Thank you for reading Love's Escape!
I'd love for you to connect with me!

Find pictures related to my books and research on Pinterest.

Get advance notice of book signings & giveaways by going to my Contact page on my website www.carriefancettpagels.com/contact and sign up in the form on the right side of the page.

Bookbub – Follow me there and be notified of upcoming releases! @CarrieFancettPagels

Follow my Facebook Author Page.

Blogs: Overcoming With God
www.OvercomingwithGod.com and
Colonial Quills www.ColonialQuills.org

Twitter @cfpagels
Instagram @carriefancettpagels
goodreads @cfpagels

James River Romances

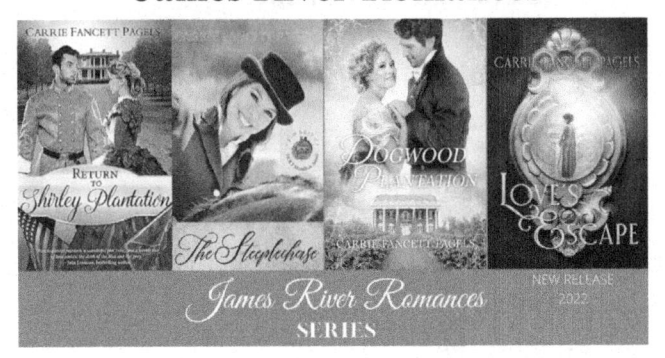

Excerpt from *Dogwood Plantation*

Prologue

Dogwood Plantation
Charles City, Virginia, 1814

Cornelia trembled in the open door to the plantation owner's bedroom, a handkerchief covering her face—not much protection against yellow fever, but something. Lee Williams lay still, paler even than Pa had been at the end, in what was about to become the Dogwood Plantation owner's deathbed.

"Miss Gill?" Lee's voice rasped like a dry corn husk scraping over a tabletop.

Her knees shook harder. She daren't go any closer. She had to think of her brother Andy, too. This pestilence spread quickly. Far too fast. She'd been summoned home from her position in Richmond only two weeks earlier but it felt nigh unto an eternity with all the illness and death. "Yes?"

"Bring… Carter… home."

Her hands joined her knees in wobbling. If she made this promise, could she live with the consequences? And how would she get to Williamsburg? She couldn't go on her own.

"Promise… me." Lee struggled to lift his head and began to cough.

She took two steps back, ready to run. Someone grabbed her shoulders and she jumped, the handkerchief slipping from her face.

"Miss Gill, you got to go get Master Carter." Nemi, the Williams's house servant quickly released Cornelia's shoulders.

"Sorry miss, but you was about to knock me plum over." The heavyset woman took two steps back and lingered in the hallway.

Cornelia covered her nose and mouth again and faced the dying man, who was only a handful of years older than herself. Lee's wife, Anne, had died only days earlier. Their passel of children were isolated in their rooms upstairs.

"I will go and get Carter." Never mind that her own father's body had just been laid in the grave, with no funeral and no words spoken over him other than what she and Andy had managed. What a terrible way to part with their beloved father.

Charles City County had never seen the likes of this outbreak of yellow fever. The epidemic struck in all classes from the wealthy, like Lee Williams and his wife, to the poor slaves in the fields. She'd pick herself up and do what she had to do.

"Nell?" Lee's light eyes pleaded. "It… wasn't me… who sent you away—"

Cornelia raised her hand, her eyes moistening at his use of her childhood nickname. "Shush, it doesn't matter now."

Lee closed his eyes.

All that pain of separation from Carter. Even with the hateful things Roger Williams had said to justify sending Cornelia to Richmond and away from Pa and Andy, this horrific yellow fever epidemic and the war had wiped away her anger at Lee and Carter's father. And anger at Carter, too, if she was honest with herself. She had to let that go. Those little boys upstairs had no one to care for them now except their Uncle Carter, and she'd not let them down.

Nemi shuffled forward. "Missy, you tell them schoonermen to take you to get Master Carter."

Yes, she could have those men who were well enough to sail take her to Williamsburg. She nodded.

"I'll take care of Master Lee." Nemi shook her head slowly. "Won't be long now, Missy."

Cornelia drew in a shuddering breath. *God, grant Lee a peaceful passage home to Glory.* "Do you think the people outside of Charles City know about the contagion? Will they even allow us in port?"

"The good Lord gonna help you bring Master Carter home, I know it in my heart." Nemi pressed a hand to her chest.

As Cornelia turned to go, she could have sworn she heard Nemi mutter, "He need to be here for you, too." Had she imagined it or had the servant spoken aloud the same words in Cornelia's own heart?

She left the house and hurried across the vast Dogwood Plantation property to her own home. She'd get her brother, Andy, and begin their journey. She didn't want to leave the grieving twelve-year-old alone.

As she approached the cabin, she spied her brother. "Oh, Andy, Mr. Lee is at the end."

Andy swiped at his tears.

"We need to go to the college and I'll need you to go into the men's dormitory for me to get Carter."

"Will you tell him, though?"

"Yes." She didn't need that duty to land on her brother's young shoulders.

They went into the cabin and gathered a few items to carry with them and headed out. An icy cloak of despair settled on Cornelia's shoulders as she and her brother hurried past the Catalpas that edged their property, the tall tree's frond-like leaves waving. The same breeze that stirred the branches should hurry them toward Williamsburg once they were aboard the schooner—and would place her face-to-face with the one man she couldn't bear to see again.

Chapter One

Williamsburg, Virginia

How did one plan a future when their world was crumbling around them? Carter Williams tapped his fingers on the long wooden table that served as his and his peers' desk, trying to focus his attention on his law professor. The College of William & Mary Law School had been his original plan—but that plan had included Cornelia Gill at his side. Since he'd spied her in Richmond several weeks earlier, her visage preoccupied his reveries.

He exhaled a slow breath. Instead of daydreaming of what he'd lost, he should spend time praying for his former crewmates still at sea.

Beside him, Ethan Randolph whispered, "Have you heard that Bonaparte might soon be defeated?"

Carter nodded in what he hoped was an imperceptible manner. He didn't need their professor shouting at him today.

Randolph, like Carter, had mustered out of the Navy with injuries. "More British ships will thus be directed toward America."

He dipped his chin slightly. He was tempted to pray about that, but God didn't seem to listen anymore. Carter rubbed his painful leg, a daily reminder of his own fragile humanity. Twenty-six years old and now disabled from serving his country. The ornamental sword they'd awarded him for bravery had done nothing to erase his injury.

Professor Danner's robes brushed Carter's arm as he strode down the aisle and paused at the next row. "Here at the second oldest institution of learning in our country, we expect law students to remain awake." A loud thwack echoed in Carter's ears. His classmate, John Bradley, awoke and jerked upright.

A sharp rap on the wooden dais startled him. "Mr. Williams, what think you of the act proposed to reexamine the Kentucky and Virginia borders?"

An image of Daniel Scott dragging Nell across the Virginia line and into Kentucky surged through Carter's mind. Sweat beaded on his forehead. "I believe it shall go forward and the Indians will be stripped of their rights." 'Twas Professor Danner's own position. If Carter were to become an elected official, how would he persuade his constituents that such a move was morally wrong?

"An intelligent fellow you are, Mr. Williams." The professor's bushy eyebrows rose as he sought other quarry. "Mr. Randolph, could you elaborate on why Mr. Williams might be correct?"

What was Daniel Scott's position on the matter? He'd left long ago and was rumored to practice law in Kentucky. What an irony that would be if the miscreant was now involved in politics. Carter unclenched the fists that he hadn't realized he had made. Daniel no longer posed a threat to himself or to Nell. Yellow fever was the Williams's enemy, not Daniel. Thankfully, his brother and sister-in-law wrote that they were taking appropriate precautions to protect themselves from the scourge.

Professor Danner pointed his stick at Bradley, who seemed quite alert now. "Give us some air in here."

Bradley rose and opened the mullioned windows on the far wall, allowing a crisp breeze to enter. As a gust filled the first-floor room, students smacked their hands down on their papers, securing them to their desks. Carter spied a dray lurching down Richmond Road adjacent to the building. He stiffened, certain he recognized the wagon as his family's own, kept at the

Williamsburg wharf. He struggled to stand, hoping to secure a better look.

Yellow-blonde curls—like corn silk—identified the driver as Cornelia Gill. A boy sat beside Nell—her brother, Andrew. His heart beat the staccato sound of a drumbeat readying for war. *Oh Lord, please no.* Someone in Carter's family must have died. He could fathom no other reason for her arrival. She wouldn't have sailed down from Charles City were it not for some grave purpose.

His legs trembling, he clutched the desktop and lowered himself into his seat.

"Mr. Williams? Are you unwell?' Professor Danner held his Elmwood pointer high.

"'Tis my family's conveyance on the road." Carter loosened his collar and dabbed at the perspiration on his forehead. "I must beg your leave, sir."

Author Bio

Carrie Fancett Pagels, "Overcoming With God" is a multi-award-winning, bestselling, multi-published Christian fiction novelist. She lives in the Historic Triangle of Virginia with her "handsome chauffeur" engineer husband, her history buff son who is also a writer, and her granddog—an Australian Kelpie.

A Yooper by birth, you'll find Carrie up at the Straits of Mackinac in the summers. The rest of the year she's in coastal Virginia, where many of her ancestors lived hundreds of years ago. Previously a psychologist for twenty-five years, Carrie's Rheumatoid Autoimmune Disease has kept her fully reliant upon God— as the Lord has helped her with her writing ministry.

Made in the USA
Columbia, SC
10 March 2022